KEPT AT THE ARGENTINE'S COMMAND

BY
LUCY ELLIS

MILLS & BOON

First Published in Great Britain 2016
By Mills & Boon, an imprint of HarperCollins*Publishers*
1 London Bridge Street, London, SE1 9GF

© 2016 Lucy Ellis

ISBN: 978-0-263-91614-0

Our policy is to use papers that are natural, renewable and recyclable
products and made from wood grown in sustainable forests. The logging
and manufacturing processes conform to the legal environmental
regulations of the country of origin.

Printed and bound in Spain
by CPI, Barcelona

KEPT AT THE ARGENTINE'S COMMAND

For my dear dad, who is 80 this year.
May he see many more stories to come.

CHAPTER ONE

ALEJANDRO NOTICED HER on boarding because she was easily the sweetest view on offer: a drop of honey on a dull day.

A slightly built girl, sitting with her long slender legs crossed at the knee, her head was bent as she read, causing her mop of artfully arranged blue-black curls, cut short at the back and longer towards the front, to topple forward around her face. She wore the highly feminised clothes of an earlier era in a way he recognised was a fashion statement.

As he made his way down the aisle towards his seat she lifted her eyes from her e-reader and they locked with his.

Those curls, he discovered, framed delicate features. She had a short upturned nose, big dark brown eyes and a mouth like a red rosebud. Her eyes widened, but there was nothing inviting in the way she looked at him. In fact her gaze dropped skittishly away. She reminded him of one of his fillies at home on the *estancia*, toeing the ground for some attention and then shying away.

He didn't mind shy—he could work with it fine.

Sure enough, her gaze swung upwards again, back for another look, a little bolder this time, and her lavish rosebud of a mouth quivered with the beginnings of a smile.

He returned her smile—the barest tilt of his mouth, because he was out of practice with the gesture. She responded by blushing and ducking her eyes back to the little screen.

He was hooked.

He was also barely in his seat before she gestured for assistance from a flight attendant. He watched in bemused interest as for the next twenty minutes Brown Eyes kept the cabin crew on their toes with a steady stream of what appeared to be trivial requests. Glasses of water, a cushion, a blanket... It was only when she began whispering furiously to the by now harassed female flight attendant that the points she'd scored with him for being pretty to look at flew out of the window.

'No, I really *cannot* move!' Her raised voice—demanding and shrill, despite the sexy French accent—had Alejandro putting down his tablet.

When the flustered flight attendant came up the aisle he leaned out and asked what the problem was.

'An elderly gentleman is finding it difficult to make the trip to the facilities, sir,' she explained, 'and we were hoping to relocate him to a closer seat.'

She didn't mention the intransigent Brown Eyes. But she was hard to miss.

Alejandro grabbed his jacket and reached up to the overhead locker.

'Not a problem,' he said, flashing the flight attendant a smile. She blushed.

Re-seated further towards the rear of the plane, he re-opened his tablet, forgot about the brunette and gave his attention to the screen.

The morning papers on his tablet didn't offer much encouragement about his destination.

When one of Russia's richest oligarchs tied the knot with a sprightly red-haired ex-showgirl in a Scottish castle it was news, and from what Alejandro had heard from the groom himself the press had already set up shop in the surrounding town and area for long-lens shots of the 'who's who' guest list.

Being one of the 'who's who' himself, he'd decided not to make a splash entering the country. In Alejandro's opinion, if you didn't want the attention, you shouldn't act as if you were somebody who needed it. Which meant he was flying commercial and driving the four-hour trip from Edinburgh to the coast a day early. The route would reportedly take him through some picturesque countryside, and he intended to cruise into Dunlosie under the radar.

Still, the hullaballoo he was surely headed for didn't inspire encouragement that this was going to be anything other than a weekend to endure.

Impatiently Alejandro tossed aside his tablet and angled his wide-shouldered frame out of his seat. He'd never been able to sit still for long.

And that was when a little cough sounded to his left and he looked down.

It was Brown Eyes.

She'd taken a few trips up and down the aisle to the 'facilities'. Either she had a little bladder problem or, more likely, she was looking for some attention.

He surveyed her coolly. Possibly not the attention she wanted.

With each trip up the aisle her step had become more rolling and he suspected she was a little drunk.

She was also considerably tall for a woman. He took a look down and found the culprits: a pair of very high-heeled turquoise shoes, ridiculously encumbered by ribbons that frothed around her trim ankles.

She in turn was gazing up at him, all brown eyes and carefully cultivated curls. Irritatingly, she was as pretty as ever.

'Pardon, m'sieur.'

Her voice sounded a little slurred. Definitely drinking.

Unimpressed, he murmured, 'Maybe you should go easy on the free liquor, *señorita*, and do us all a favour.'

She blinked. *'Pardonnez-moi?'*

'You heard me.'

For a moment she seemed to be utterly lost for words. Then she screwed up her nose and stamped her foot.

It took a great deal of his self-control not to smile.

'Why don't you move out of the way instead of bullying

people?' she demanded, her French accent doing an excellent job on the precise English she used.

He ran his gaze insolently from the top of her shiny curls to the ribbons cascading over her pointy shoes and back to everything in between.

The in between was rather sweetly distributed...

She backed up a bit, but he wasn't letting her get away scot-free.

'You're quite a piece of work, aren't you, *chica*?' he drawled.

'I beg your pardon?'

'There are fourteen people in First Class today,' he spelt out. 'Your name isn't written on the plane and the cabin crew aren't your personal galley slaves. How about cutting us all some slack?'

Her eyes fell away from his. 'I don't know what you're talking about,' she mumbled. 'Now, move, why don't you?'

It was all he needed. 'Make me.'

Her chin came up and her rosebud of a mouth dropped open.

He was slightly surprised himself. He didn't, as a rule, hassle women. Especially silly little girls who needed to grow up.

For a moment he thought those big brown eyes were going to fill with ready tears. She certainly seemed on the brink of something.

So he moved.

Just.

She made a very French *'ouf'* sound of disapproval, averted her face and stalked back to her seat. Once more in charge of herself. Self-interest on two legs.

Only then she ruined it with an almost furtive look back over her shoulder, as if to make sure he wasn't following her.

The first finger of doubt touched his shoulder.

He'd made a few hard conclusions drawn from not much.

But life had taught him to pay attention to what people told you by their actions, not their words.

She had barely reached her seat when he heard her give a soft cry.

Alejandro turned—fast.

'*Non*, leave those things alone!'

He relaxed, a little surprised at his own reflexes when he didn't even like the woman. She was back to making everyone's life a misery.

She followed this up with a hushed volley of what sounded like furious French, but she was speaking so fast it was hard to tell. And all of it was directed at the poor steward, who was tidying up the clutter she had accumulated around her.

Heads emerged into the aisle.

Alejandro swung back into his seat and checked his phone. He was done with her.

There was a message from the groom.

Change in plans. Do me a favour and pick up a bridesmaid on your way in. Answers to Lulu Lachaille. Exiting Flight 338 at Gate Four. She's precious cargo. If you lose her, Gigi will cut off my balls and call off the wedding.

Alejandro briefly considered texting back *no*, even as he kissed his peaceful drive goodbye. Weddings were his worst nightmare. Spending four hours in a car with a chatty little bridesmaid didn't exactly float his boat.

Although the bridal party was bound to be stocked with leggy showgirls, so it might not be that bad...

Dios.

He stuck his head out into the aisle, only to find that the French Miss was leaning out too.

She had the open, hopeful expression of a cartoon princess awaiting aid from one of her magical creatures.

Then she saw him, and her expression darkened and her eyes diminished to dark cat-like slits.

As if on cue a flight attendant appeared at her side, with still water and what appeared to be some form of medication.

A headache? It just got better and better.

He flipped open the attachment Khaled had sent him, but a part of him already knew what he was going to see.

He didn't know whether to laugh or groan.

A dark-eyed angel gazed seriously up at him from the screen.

She was really quite something.

He angled a resigned glance down the aisle. The only problem was—she was also *her*.

CHAPTER TWO

MAKE ME?

Trotting across the plane's bridge, Lulu fumed. It was at the forefront of her mind to make a complaint to the airline.

Women should be free to fly the skies unmolested by hulking great brutes who thought they occupied the high moral ground.

Although she guessed he *did*.

She guessed he didn't think much of her because she hadn't given up her seat.

Lulu's heart plummeted.

She'd seen the looks on the other passengers' faces and knew they all felt the same way, but what could she have done?

The cabin crew had been apprised of her condition and had been considerate with all of her requests. Only one of them clearly hadn't got the memo regarding her flying issues, and when she'd been asked to move to another seat her feet had turned to lead.

Just the idea of shifting everything, when she'd created a safe little space for herself around her seat, had been too overwhelming. She might as well have been asked to leap from the plane!

By the time she was waiting at the luggage carousel Lulu was no longer fuming but feeling utterly wretched.

What kind of a person didn't give up their seat to a sick, elderly man?

Perhaps she should have heeded her mother's advice and brought someone with her? Lulu worried. Then none of this would have happened.

But how was she to have anything like a normal life if

she always had to take people along with her? She was a full-grown woman—not an invalid! She could do better than this. She stood up straighter. She could try harder...

She *was* trying harder.

Ever since she had tried to break up her best friend's relationship six months ago she'd been actively trying to do better.

She'd found a different therapist from the one her parents had arranged and got a proper diagnosis. At least she knew now that her actions with Gigi had been motivated by separation anxiety and were a symptom of her illness.

But it would have been too easy to use her condition as an excuse for her behaviour—lying to bring Gigi back home just so she could feel safer, and in the process trying to steal her best friend's joy with a man who'd proved to be the best thing that had ever happened to her. Who *did* something like that? A boxed-in, desperate person, that was who—and she didn't want to be that person any more.

That was why she was in the process of turning her entire life upside down.

She had signed up for a course in costume design and she now had ambitions for a life beyond the cabaret.

It had been that single act which had given her the necessary self-confidence to imagine she could undertake this flight on her own.

But all her preparations for taking the flight hadn't factored in a big, macho stranger, cornering her in the aisle on her way back from the facilities, where most of the contents of her stomach had gone down the toilet.

'A piece of work', he'd called her. As if she were defective—something she'd worked hard with her therapist to convince herself she wasn't.

Lulu realised her hand was shaking as she pointed out her luggage to the nice airport attendant who had volunteered to help her.

That was something that man from the plane could have been—helpful rather than being horrible to her.

Oh, forget him, she told herself briskly. *He's probably forgotten all about you!*

To be honest, as she made her way out into Arrivals with her stick-and-stop trolley, she was feeling a bit desperate, and was looking forward to seeing her fellow bridesmaids, Susie and Trixie. They at least would provide a buffer against the rest of the world.

Right now Lulu didn't think she could face anything more challenging.

Only ten minutes later she was still scanning the crowd anxiously and wondering if she was even going to get to the castle before Gigi said *I do.*

She had her phone out to track down the other girls when she was nudged by a new influx of people streaming around her and jostled backwards into a warm, hard body. Incredibly hard. Masculine, judging by the size, the solidity and the weight of the strong hands that settled around her shoulders to steady her.

He said something and Lulu froze.

She recognised that voice.

Dieu, it was the bully from the plane.

Run—run!

But her legs had gone to water. As much as she reminded herself that hostile men didn't scare her any more—she had rights…she was protected under the law—she still felt incredibly vulnerable. And she hated that feeling. She was trying so hard to be strong.

Which didn't explain why she'd fastened her gaze on his wide sensual mouth, noticing the shadow along his jaw where he'd clearly shaved this morning and would probably need to shave again later. He was *very* masculine.

Lulu reminded herself that she didn't like masculine men. She didn't like the way they pushed and shoved and shouldered their way through the world and got away with things through intimidation. They made her nervous. Only this man didn't exactly make her nervous—he made her something else.

It was the *something else* she was struggling with now, even knowing what a bully he was.

He was also gorgeously tall and broad-shouldered, with a stunning face—all cheekbones and sensuous mouth and golden-brown eyes that looked magnetic against the olive tint of his skin.

His tousled chestnut-brown hair was so thick and silky-looking her fingers just itched to touch it. She made fists of her hands.

She didn't like him, and he was looking at her as if he didn't like her very much either.

Good, it was mutual. The not liking, that was.

So what if he looked like…? Well, he looked like Gary Cooper. In his rakish early career, when he'd picked up and slept with every starlet who wasn't nailed down.

Not Gregory Peck, though. Gregory Peck was reliable and stalwart and…*decent*. He would never insult a woman.

Stop staring at him. Stop comparing him to Golden Age Hollywood movie stars.

'*Buenas tardes, señorita,*' he said, in a voice that made him sound as if he was making an indecent proposal to her. 'I believe you're looking for me.'

Lulu automatically repressed the responsive curl of smoke in her lower belly raised by the sound of his deep and sexy Spanish accent.

No, no, *no*—he would be lighting no fires in *her* valley.

She drew herself up. 'I certainly am not.'

Alejandro was tempted to shrug and walk away, and let the little *princesita* discover the hard way that he wasn't trying to pick her up. But in the end he had a duty to perform for a friend and she was it.

She continued to regard him as if he would spring at her, so he extended his hand.

'Alejandro du Crozier.'

She looked at his hand as if he'd pulled a gun on her.

'Please leave me alone,' she said, a touch furtively, and turned a rigid shoulder on him.

'I'm not trying to pick you up, *señorita*.' He tried again with what he considered was remarkable patience.

Her narrow back told him what she thought about *that* claim.

'You clearly didn't get the message. *Lulu*,' he added dryly.

The use of her name had the intended effect. She peered at him cautiously over her shoulder, reminding Alejandro absurdly of a timid creature sticking its head out of a hole.

'H-how do you know my name?'

He folded his arms.

'I'm your ride,' he said flatly.

'My *ride*?'

As soon as she said it Lulu felt herself go red.

She didn't have a dirty mind—truly she didn't. She was always the last one to get the blue jokes that ran like quicksilver around the dressing room before shows at L'Oiseau Bleu, the Parisian cabaret where she danced in the chorus, but right now something seemed to have gone wrong with her. It had something to do with the way he looked at her— as if he knew exactly how she looked in her underwear.

Earlier he'd looked at her as if she was a bug he'd wanted to squash. Better to think about being the bug.

To her embarrassment she stepped back and almost tripped over her hand luggage. His hand shot out and grasped her elbow, saving her from a fall.

'Careful, *bella*,' he said, his warm breath brushing the top of her ear.

Her knees went to jelly.

She tried to tug herself free, confused. 'Will you let me pass?'

'*Señorita,*' he said, holding her in place, 'I am Alejandro du Crozier, and I will be driving you to the wedding.'

Her eyes flew to his. He knew about the wedding? That meant he was a guest too.

'But Susie and Trixie are driving me to the wedding.' As soon as she said it she realised those plans had possibly changed.

'I know nothing of these women. I only know of you.' His expression said that this wasn't making his day.

Which was fine, Lulu decided. That made two of them. She gave another tug and he let go.

'I don't make a habit of going off with strange men, Mr—Mr—'

He pulled out his phone and held it up in front of her. She peered at the message on the screen and then looked at him in mute astonishment.

'*Khaled* sent you?'

He gave that question the look it deserved. But he didn't have to stand so close, did he? And he didn't have to look at her mouth as if there was something about it that interested him. She most definitely didn't have *anything* to interest him.

Weirdly, her heart was hammering.

His amber eyes, lushly lashed, met hers with a splintering intensity.

'Unless you're interested in walking, *chica*, I suggest you come with me now.'

He didn't give her a chance to object. He was walking away. He clearly expected her to follow him.

Lulu stared after him.

He was the rudest man.

She found herself struggling one-handed with her stick-and-stop trolley, her hand luggage banging painfully against her leg.

She most certainly was *not* travelling with him in a car for three or four hours.

She would find a taxi.

She would entrust her person and her luggage to a man she had *paid* to do the task—not one who thought he was doing her a big favour.

Money was a woman's greatest ally and protection. She knew it to be so. Without money her mother had been unable to escape her violent father.

Even now, with her mother blissfully married to another man, Lulu pushed her to keep her own bank account and manage her own money. Money gave you options. Lulu lifted her chin. Right now her own personal bank account gave her the ability to pay her way to Dunlosie Castle.

But when she emerged from the building it was into an overcast Edinburgh day. There was a light rain falling and Lulu stopped to retrieve her umbrella, opening it against the elements and peering about. She spotted the cab rank but there was a queue.

All right, sometimes those options a woman had weren't optimal, but there was no help for it.

She pushed resolutely in that direction, aware that her pretty harlequin seamed stockings were receiving tiny splashes of dirty water with each step from the washback beneath the wheels of her trolley. The fact that she felt depleted from withstanding her own anxieties in the air for the last couple of hours wasn't helping. Lulu wanted nothing more than to be warm and comfortable inside a car, with her shoes off, watching this bad weather through a windscreen.

Maybe she'd been a little hasty...

Which was when she saw the lovingly restored red vintage Jaguar.

The passenger side window came rolling down.

'Get in,' he instructed.

CHAPTER THREE

LULU KNEW SHE had a decision to make.

She lifted her umbrella to take another look at the queue. Then she looked at her 'ride'.

Hot and sexy and far too full of himself—and he had looked at her as if she was a bug.

Her pride pushed to the fore. She was *not* climbing into a car with a man who didn't even have the decency to open the door for her. And what about her luggage?

Lulu was tempted in that moment to phone her parents, who would be arriving at the castle tonight. But how would that look? And she couldn't lean on Gigi this weekend of all weekends.

She gasped as another splash of muddy water, this time from passing pedestrians, hit her shoes and saw the mud now attached to her sadly limp blue ribbons. Her pride wavered.

Dieu, she knew she'd regret this.

She grabbed her trolley and pushed it towards the back end of the car.

It was really completely unfair, but frankly she'd be a fool if she passed this up.

She stood there. In the rain. Waiting.

He took his time.

Lulu narrowed her eyes on his languid stroll around to the boot, all shoulders and confident attitude, looking infinitely rugged and male and capable.

But she knew differently. Knew how a sturdy exterior could mask all kinds of weaknesses and flaws.

She'd bet this man had plenty. For one thing, he didn't like women. The things he'd said to her on the plane…

The way he'd curled his lip at her shoes… She'd seen the way he'd looked at them. He had no idea how secure these shoes made her feel. She stamped one of them, because he was making her wait deliberately.

'Open the boot, would you?'

He looked her up and down. She wasn't going to apologise for her rudeness. He needed to know she was onto him.

All the same, she took a shuffling step backwards.

She drew herself up, happily over six feet in her shoes, but still gallingly forced to tip up her chin to look him in the eye.

With a half-smile, as if he knew what she was doing, he unlocked the boot, and Lulu was mollified—and a little relieved—when without a word he began hauling her luggage inside.

He handled the matching powder-blue cases as if they weighed nothing. The problem was he was tossing them into the boot as if he was shifting hay bales.

Lulu made a sound of dismay, but from the look he gave her she was a little afraid he might haul her in there too if she said something.

It was only when he looked about to launch her carpet bag after the cases that she jumped and threw herself bodily in front of him to prevent certain shattering.

'*Doux Jésus*, stop!'

He held off, but the look on his face told her he was unimpressed—which was pretty rich, given he was the one destroying her property!

'It contains the crystal I've brought as a wedding gift. For Gigi—and Khaled,' she added, grudgingly.

'Crystal?'

'Goblets…tableware. Crystal.'

He continued to stare at her, as if she'd announced she was giving them a horse and cart.

Lulu inhaled a breath. She held out her arms. 'Give that to me.'

He complied, but she wasn't expecting him to step right up to her. She was suddenly more aware of him than ever, and inhaled his aftershave—something woodsy that mingled with the scent of his own skin. It was attractively male in a way she wasn't used to.

Confused and flustered, Lulu looked up.

She encountered his firm chin and the sensuous line of his mouth, which only made her feel more unsettled.

He had a faint frown on his face and she suspected she mirrored it.

She turned her back on him to lodge the bag carefully between two cases to prevent it being bounced around.

Rude, ignorant, appalling, macho jerk.

He waited until she'd stepped back to lower the boot. She waited patiently by the passenger door with her umbrella. But he abruptly headed for the driver's side of the car.

'The "macho jerk" wants you to get in the car,' he said flatly as he yanked open his door.

Lulu realised two things in that moment. One, she'd spoken her thoughts aloud, and, two, he wasn't going to open her door.

Given he had all her luggage now locked up inside his car, she didn't have much choice, but she cursed herself for her weakness. She should have waited for a cab.

As if to remind her why she'd made her choice, the rain began to pelt harder.

Why is this happening to me?

She closed her umbrella and opened the door herself.

'Try not to drip on the upholstery,' he shot at her as she lodged her furled umbrella at her feet.

Distinctly queasy with the added tension, Lulu looked around in desperation. Where did he expect her to put it?

'Here.' He took it from her hand and laid it on the coat he'd tossed on the back seat.

Alejandro then turned back to discover that instead of

buckling herself in she had shoved the door open further, so that the rain had begun to slant in.

His temper snapped. 'Close that damn door!'

She looked for a moment as if she was going to jump right out of the car.

And then she leaned forward and began to dry retch miserably into the gutter.

He wrenched open his door and cut around the car to find her bent double.

He hunkered down. The face she lifted was bone-white. This she couldn't fake. She clearly wasn't well, and he suspected he'd got some things wrong. He produced a handkerchief to blot her mouth and soak up the tears that were sliding down her cheeks.

If she'd been hoping for some sympathy it was effective. The big glistening eyes, the silent tears, how fragile she suddenly looked beneath her showy outfit—as if she was trying to shrink into invisibility within it...

He put his hands around her shoulders to help her back into the car and out of the rain, but her response took him off guard. Her arms shot out and she instantly had them wrapped around his neck as tenaciously as a strangling vine.

He was enveloped in the scent of her, and he wondered for a second if this was her clumsy attempt at a pass. Only the feel of her rapid heartbeat told him she was scared. It was like holding a small nervous bird to his chest—as if what she was feeling was too big for her slight body. And yet what had she to be scared of?

She was overwrought—that was all, he told himself, and possibly a little the worse for wear from her in-flight tippling.

A better question was how had he come to be the only man in Scotland who was saddled with the job of delivering a vodka-wilted bridesmaid to their shared destination?

It had to be vodka, because he couldn't smell any alcohol on her. All he smelt were those cottage violets—and something warmer and real that was just *her*.

He tentatively rubbed her back, as he would one of the young kids on the *estancia* who had taken a fall from a horse and had the wind knocked out of them, and tried to ignore the fact that she was an incredibly appealing full-grown female with her breasts pushed up against his chest.

'I don't think I'll be sick again,' she confided miserably.

She hadn't actually done anything other than spit up a little bile, but he didn't doubt her suffering. She looked more miserable than a human being should.

'Please don't tell anybody about this,' she said in a muffled voice against his neck.

It was a strange request, but she was obviously serious about it.

He cleared his throat. 'Come on, let's strap you in. Are you all right to travel?'

She nodded, allowing him to help her.

He went around to the boot to grab a bottle of water from the chiller. He yanked the screw lid off for her and when he offered it to her she took a few grateful sips.

'Okay now?' he asked gruffly.

'I'm sorry,' she said huskily, swallowing deeply and refusing to meet his eyes. 'It won't happen again.'

He drove the keys into the ignition.

'Do you want to stop for coffee? Get something in your stomach?'

She shuddered. 'I can't think of anything worse.'

'It might sober you up.'

Her eyes flashed his way in confusion. 'I *am* sober.'

He gave her an old-fashioned look.

'I am not drunk. I have not been drinking.'

'You can deny it if you want, *querida*. It doesn't change the fact you were stumbling all over that flight, your words were a little slurry and you've just been sick.'

She looked at him in horror, her knuckles white around

the bottle. 'I wasn't— That's you— I mean, nobody else thought that—'

Lulu tried to control her shaking because it wasn't helping her case.

'Maybe I should just find a taxi,' she said, deeply humiliated, and distressed as she sloshed some of the water on her skirt. Although getting out of this car was the last thing she felt up to doing. 'This isn't working for me and it's clearly not working for you.'

'Look,' he said, keeping the car idling while he took the bottle from her hands, lidded it and tossed it onto the back seat. 'In my experience nobody likes to be confronted with their behaviour while under the influence. You had a few drinks on the flight…they didn't agree with you. I'm not judging.'

'Yes, you *are* judging,' she burst out unhappily. 'And nobody thought I was drunk.'

'No, probably not—they were too busy thinking what a pain in the arse you were to fly with.'

Her chin wobbled. 'Do you get something out of insulting me?'

'*Sí*, it takes the edge off.'

She stared at him. He'd silenced her. Good. The truth was she still looked very pale, and he didn't want to argue with her any more.

'If you must know,' she said, clearly unable or unwilling to let this go, 'I had some analgesics on the plane on an empty stomach and they disagreed with me. They're to blame.'

Alejandro was ready to dismiss this out of hand, only then he remembered the medication he'd seen delivered to her.

'Well, that was stupid,' he said.

He ignored the wounded look on her face. She could save it. He'd been manipulated by women who made this one look like a rank amateur. Besides, he wasn't playing

Sir Galahad to her fair maiden. Been there, done that—had the divorce papers to prove it. The problem was she was already getting to him.

He swung the car out into the traffic. 'Almost as stupid as not giving up your seat on the flight,' he reiterated.

Lulu realised she was cornered. How on earth did she answer *that*?

'It's not your business,' she muttered, looking away.

There was no way she could tell him that whatever had been in her stomach had ended up in the plane toilet, because that was going to lead to more questions.

Questions with answers that had nothing whatsoever to do with him.

It was her private business. Her mother had drummed that into her years ago.

'If you weren't drunk there's nowhere to hide, *querida*. I'm sorry you're not feeling well. But you behaved like a spoilt brat. Forgive me if I choose to treat you like one.'

Lulu wanted to die of shame.

'You're an awful man,' she muttered, 'I hope we have nothing to do with each other this weekend at the castle.'

'Sweetheart, you took the words out of my mouth.'

CHAPTER FOUR

THEY STOPPED TO fuel up the car after a couple of hours on the road. Lulu wound down her window and saw a newspaper headline behind the glass of the service station window: *Celebrity Wedding. Oligarch Brings in Private Army of Security.*

It was a little daunting to realise she was heading into all that.

The other daunting reality was striding back towards the car. His superbly fit and powerful frame was gloved in an understated but clearly expensive set of dark trousers and a navy shirt. *Like a man who went on secret missions with the armed forces and climbed walls without ropes, just using his weapon of a body as all the equipment he required.*

Lulu looked away.

Ah, *oui*, this was her new little problem. She had discovered now she felt physically better that she was responding to that Latin machismo thing some women went a little silly over. She might not have a boyfriend as such, but she did have hormones.

She really needed to make a big effort to curb her imagination.

People were looking his way as he approached the car. So maybe she wasn't the only one. She had to admit he had the impervious aura of confidence that belonged to someone for whom the small stuff of life was taken care of. She imagined Alejandro du Crozier rarely fuelled up his own car, although he'd taken care of it easily enough.

She had watched him do it through the side mirror—watched him sticking the petrol gun into the tank. There was something about a man's broad forearm, a chunk of watch, a powerful wrist and a strong hand gripping the nozzle that put all sorts of erotic images into a woman's head.

Admittedly they were images mostly gleaned from books she'd read. Her personal notebook of erotic experiences was fairly limited.

Alejandro tossed a wrapped sandwich onto her lap as he eased in beside her and turned the engine over.

'Ham salad. It's not much, but it should tide you over until we reach Dunlosie.'

Lulu wondered if this was him thawing towards her. Whatever it was, it was a thoughtful gesture. 'Thank you,' she said uncertainly, and busied herself with unwrapping her sandwich.

She could feel his eyes on her.

'Would you like half?' she offered.

Alejandro had bought the sandwich with an eye to her turning up her pert little nose at plastic-wrapped food. His preconceptions took a solid hit.

'I had a king's breakfast,' he said shortly. 'Eat up.'

Lulu gave an internal sigh. So much for the thaw.

Half an hour up the road, Alejandro flipped his phone onto speaker.

A male voice began to speak in Spanish, and Alejandro replied in the same language.

Lulu found herself transfixed by the deep, mellifluous quality of his voice as he spoke his own language. Then a Scot's voice came on the line.

'We're pleased to have you here in Edinburgh, Mr du Crozier. Congratulations on captaining South America to that win in Palermo. It warms a Scotsman's heart to see the English floundering on a field.'

Lulu's head snapped around at that. *What was this?*

Alejandro chuckled. 'No problem at all,' he said easily in his smooth, deep voice. 'It was a good match.'

Lulu felt as if she'd had the rug pulled out from under

her. Where had *this* come from? The smile, the ease, the charm?

'We will be sending our principal to you tomorrow, at your convenience and we'll give you an aerial viewing of the property. Will it be just you, Mr du Crozier?'

'Possibly one other.' Alejandro glanced her way. 'Two o'clock looks good.'

As he ended the call Lulu told herself not to make any enquiries—she would only look nosey.

'I'm looking at property while I'm here,' he said, his eyes on the road. 'I'm thinking of investing in a golf course. It's on a picturesque strip of land along the coast near Dunlosie.'

He didn't look like a golfer. Although she suspected those broad shoulders and strong arms could hit a golf ball to the moon and back.

'Do you play golf professionally?' she ventured. When he raised an eyebrow she added hurriedly, so that she didn't look stupid, 'That man said something about you captaining a team?'

He smiled slightly. 'Polo. I captained South America.' He was watching her as if gauging her reaction. 'It received some press coverage.'

Vaguely his name stirred a memory. She rather thought she ought to know it.

'I have a little fame, Lulu.'

He must have read her frown.

'Ah, *oui*.'

She tried not to look curious or impressed, or as if she cared. He was smiling to himself, and she wanted to tell him she didn't care if he was famous, or who he knew. It wasn't as if she was angling to spend any time with him when they reached the castle. She wasn't *interested* in him. He was just transport.

She leaned forward and rummaged in her bag.

It was almost a relief to have her phone in her hand and

something to concentrate on other than the magnetism of the man beside her.

He flicked on the sound system.

'Is that necessary?'

Alejandro spared her a glance. 'It passes the time.'

'I'm trying to do some work.'

'Games on your phone?'

'Wedding plans. See.' She held it up but he kept his eye on the wet road.

'Isn't that the bride and groom's prerogative?'

'I'm maid of honour,' she said proudly. 'I have responsibilities.'

Alejandro thumped the wheel with the heel of his hand.

'What's wrong?' she demanded.

'Santa Maria,' he said under his breath, and after a moment began to chuckle.

'What's so funny?'

When he kept laughing her expression took on a look of bafflement, and for a moment she looked very young and decidedly adorable.

He didn't want her to look adorable. He took another look. Definitely adorable. No wonder she had entitlement issues. He doubted there was a man alive who could resist those big brown eyes or her air of fragility.

It would bother him. If he was considering taking this anywhere. But since the day he had learned he'd inherited everything, in the form of the *estancia* and all the debts his father had collected, and gained nothing but his mother's endless demands for more money, his wife's desire for freedom and the everlasting dissatisfaction of his disinherited sisters he'd carried around the feeling that he'd let them all down.

Fragile women required a lot more than he was able to give.

'I want to know why you're laughing at me,' she insisted.

'I'm going to kill him.'

'Kill who? What are you talking about?'

'Fate. The universe. Khaled Kitaev.'

'You're not making any sense.'

'I'm *padrino de boda, querida.*'

She had a blank look on her face that made him want to spin this out a little longer, because watching her lose a little of that tight composure was almost worth the hassle.

He relented and filled her in. 'Best man.'

She dropped her device and it slithered through her satin skirt and thumped at her feet.

'You *can't* be!'

'I am.'

'But we don't like each other.' She clamped her mouth shut, as if she couldn't believe that had just slipped out.

No, maybe not, but he'd just discovered he *did* like her. She might be spoiled and self-centred, but he lived in a world where most women fell at his feet.

Lulu Lachaille would fall, if he applied the right pressure here and there, but she wasn't going to trip herself up.

She might just be what he was looking for this weekend after all.

Distraction from the spectacle that was a wedding, where everybody mouthed belief in fidelity and love ever after but nobody in his world practised it.

Although he had to admit Khaled and Gigi did seem to be that rarest of unions—a couple who genuinely liked one another.

And he liked Gigi's little friend, with her pretty curls and her rosebud pout and her French girl's way of looking as if she was bored and it was his job to entertain her.

'I wouldn't say I don't like you,' he said, checking out her pretty knees, just visible under the froth of her netted underskirt. Her hands went there immediately, smoothing it down.

'Not in that way,' she said crossly. 'I don't want you to

like me that way at all. I mean in a *platonic* sense. In a maid of honour and best man *duty* sense.'

'Now I'm a duty? Careful, *querida*, you'll damage my ego.'

'I doubt that,' she said repressively.

He grinned.

She looked decidedly flummoxed.

'You'll need to make an effort, then,' she blurted out almost defensively.

'I intend to.'

Lulu tried to ignore the fact that she felt hot all over. Was he *flirting* with her?

'I'm serious. You'll have to be polite to me so people don't notice anything's wrong.'

But something *is* wrong, thought Lulu, checking him out surreptitiously. Why did he have that sexy half-smile sitting at the corner of his mouth? He kept looking at her and she didn't want him to look at her. It made her feel most unlike herself.

'The best man has duties with the maid of honour,' she persevered staunchly, feeling as if she was drowning in something and holding on to talk of the wedding as a life buoy.

'*Sí*, I believe he does.'

Not those kind of duties. The thought just appeared in her head. It should have embarrassed her, and her heart was racing crazily, but a big part of her was actually enjoying the attention.

Alejandro du Crozier was flirting with her and she wasn't diving for the nearest manhole to escape.

Probably because she knew she wouldn't be seeing him again after this weekend.

It wasn't as if he was going to ask her out. This was just a straightforward few hours in a car together, and then there was the weekend... Maybe it would be okay just to

pretend for a few hours that she was normal and he was...
interested?

That was when the car gave a bit of a lurch, and the
sound of rubber dragging on the road had Lulu gripping
her seat.

Alejandro said something filthy in Spanish even as he
braked, and all the heat that had been building between
them dissipated with the reality of the car coming to a stop
at the side of the road.

Lulu forgot how much she'd been enjoying herself as
her old friend panic set in and she looked around wildly.
'What's going on? Why are we stopping?'

There was no way she was getting out *here*, in the middle of nowhere!

'It's a flat. The back left tyre is shot.'

At least it wasn't electrical. Lulu slumped a little in her
seat. She could stay where she was, safe and sound, and
it wouldn't take too long. She could manage this. But she
needed to dial down the panic. She cast about for something
to pin her focus to in the car and remembered her phone.

In the silence that followed she glanced up, only to find
he was watching her. She really didn't want him to notice
how nervous she was. 'Well, fix it,' she said defensively,
before returning her attention to the screen.

Fix it?

Alejandro cut the engine and eased back in his seat to
take a good look at what exactly he had on his hands.

One hundred and thirty pounds, at a guess, of Paris-bred
entitlement—and he damn well wasn't her mechanic. His
gaze dwelt on her soft, petulant mouth. Although there was
something he wouldn't mind fixing.

He reached across, plucked her phone from her hands
and tossed it onto the back seat.

Time to take the edge off his distracting sexual interest in her.

Lulu gave him a puzzled look. He'd sort that out for her too.

He leaned in.

Her eyes widened, her breath came short, but she didn't exactly push him away as he slid his fingers through the astonishingly silky weight of curls behind her head and fitted his mouth with practised ease to hers.

Her muffled yelp gave him the opportunity to invade her warm mouth. He had planned to make this quick. He didn't linger where he wasn't wanted. Only Lulu wasn't struggling, and she made no attempt to push him away. Instead her hands unfolded over his shoulders and then, almost tentatively, she was kissing him back.

He let her.

This wasn't about proving a point any more.

Her hand stroked gently against his shoulder as she moved her mouth sensuously against his.

She was seducing him. And it was working. His body was suddenly as hard as a pick axe.

Which was inconvenient, given neither of them could do anything about it right now, in a broken-down car on the side of a quiet Scottish road.

Sí, not one of his smarter moves.

He began to think about leaping into ice holes in Reykjavik, of losing to a lesser team, about the very real possibility that a photo of him making out like a teenager with this girl might all too easily end up on the internet.

But what *should* have killed his desire stone-dead was the wave of tenderness that came over him as she drew away and hid her face in his neck in a gesture of embarrassment that oddly, crazily, had a rush of male protectiveness surging up from nowhere.

He found himself stroking the back of her neck, the urge to be affectionate with her amazingly strong.

Fragile, he told himself again. *She's fragile.*

Lulu was aware that Alejandro was moving away from

her and she had nowhere to hide. One minute she'd been trying to control her panic, the next she'd been tipped into something she hadn't had a lot of in her twenty-three years—the feel, the scent, the excitement of a man kissing her. And not just *any* man. *This* man. This very masculine man, who knew exactly what he was doing.

Her heart had slammed against her chest as his mouth had slid against hers. It had been the most invigorating experience of her life.

She waited for him to say something, because for the life of her she had nothing. Zero.

'All fixed now,' he said, dropping the words into her lap as if he'd tossed her his hotel room key.

It wasn't his words but the deliberation with which he wielded them that had her gaze flying to meet his. And then his meaning became clear.

Fixed? Lulu floundered with the concept. He'd done it on purpose? He hadn't been carried away like her at all?

Mon Dieu, what a little fool she was.

Her heart was still galloping like a wild horse, and now it picked up pace for all the wrong reasons.

She was aware of him watching her from beneath hooded eyes…aware that he now knew a great deal more about her than he had minutes ago. More than any man knew, to her deep embarrassment. And he'd set her up. He'd done it to humiliate her.

Her hand shot out but he caught it before she found her target. 'No slapping, *mi belleza*.'

Alejandro watched the struggle on her face and, as much as he welcomed the status quo between them being lodged once more in place, he knew he'd acted like a bastard.

And that was when he heard it. The rumble.

His attention moved across to the side rear-vision mirror and he saw what was coming.

Lulu wrenched her wrist out of his hold and wiped her

mouth with the back of her hand to give him the message. 'You're *never* to do that again.'

'Fine.' He kept his eye on what was coming.

'There's a name for men who force themselves on unwilling women.' She addressed him directly, unbuckling her belt.

That had his attention.

'I didn't use any force, *querida.*' He was frowning at her. 'You were with me the whole way. It's called chemistry.'

'I know what it's called.' She opened her door.

'Where the hell are you going?' he growled, not liking her spin on this.

'Somewhere far away from *you.*' Which was when she gave a shriek and slammed the door shut again.

Around them a sea of black-faced sheep surged, like something out of a biblical plague. The car rocked slightly with the force.

'I probably should have mentioned that,' Alejandro drawled, winding down his window. 'We've got company.'

CHAPTER FIVE

I'M GOING TO DIE.

Lulu went stiff as a board as all around her the road just seemed to fill up with sheep.

'Welcome to Scotland,' said Alejandro, propping one arm casually on the door, as if floating in a sea of sheep happened regularly in Argentina.

A whimper had buried itself at the base of her throat, and she just knew that if she opened her mouth it would come out and humiliate her. But, really, how much worse could it get?

She had to speak. To make something happen.

'Drive, why don't you?' she hissed at him a little desperately.

'Where?' He gestured at the woolly tide. 'This is Scotland, *chica*. Here we give way to sheep.'

Lulu didn't know if this was true or just more of him tormenting her. She suspected a little of both.

'Besides,' he added, 'the back tyre's shot.'

Forget the tyre! *She* was shot. Her mouth pulsed from his kiss and her body felt oddly light, but that might be shock setting in. Because those big, woolly mammoths with their black faces were turning her tummy to cold liquid and her pulse was going so fast she thought she might pass out.

This was worse than a two-hour flight from Paris to Edinburgh, or letting a man she had only known for a few hours at most plant a kiss on her.

This was her worst nightmare.

Because she couldn't escape. And the knowledge that she was only inches away from a full meltdown in front of this man was probably the only thing keeping her upright and frozen in her seat.

She knew she should never have got in this car with him.

She had no more control over her anxieties than she'd possessed this morning before the flight, when she'd knelt over the porcelain bowl at home in her flat and lost her breakfast.

Dieu, what if she was sick again? In this car? He wouldn't be kind. There wasn't a kind bone in his body.

There was a click, and Lulu realised he'd opened his door.

'What are you doing?' she almost shrieked.

He looked surprised by her vehemence. 'I'm going to have a word with the farmer,' he said mildly. 'It's a damn sight better than sitting here. Come on.'

'No!' She clutched hold of his arm.

'Or we could stay here and neck like a couple of teenagers,' he said dryly.

Lulu let him go in a flash, and discovered she really was between a rock and a hard place.

'Come on,' he said more patiently. 'Stretch your legs.'

Lulu flailed around for a reason not to—any reason. 'I don't like sheep. They're smelly, and—' she cast about for something...anything '—and I'll wreck my shoes.'

He gave her a look that in all honesty she knew her comments deserved and her toes curled under inside said shoes. The last of the confident, take-on-the-world Lulu died inside her. The Lulu who had sprung to life in his arms and kissed him back barely had time to take flight. She was back to being useless.

What made it worse was that he shrugged, as if it didn't matter to him either way, which she guessed it didn't.

'Suit yourself, *chica*.' He swung open his door and Lulu realised he was serious.

He was also back to calling her *chica*.

Lulu watched in tense dismay as he took off in easy

strides down the road, all shoulders and masculine confidence, shouting out something to the two men driving the sheep. Obviously magic words, given they waited for him and then stood around conversing with him like old friends.

She sat forward, her nose almost to the glass, wondering what on earth they had to say to one another that was causing such a friendly, animated discussion. When he spoke to *her* all he did was rile her and growl. Or kiss her. Lulu hesitantly touched her mouth and swore she could still feel tingling.

A loud, long bleat sounded over her right shoulder and Lulu almost shot through the roof, any thoughts of kissing him shattering into a thousand pieces.

To her relief he came strolling back to the car. He leaned in.

'Some of the connections are probably loose, I could fix it but it might happen again. Tell you what, I'll give road assistance a call and organize another car. There's a pub just down the road. We can wander down and wait for them there.'

Lulu knew this was the moment a normal, sensible woman would confess her problem. She would explain why there was no way she could get out, due to her difficulties, and they would come up with a solution together.

Only there wasn't really a solution, was there? And right now she wasn't a sensible woman. She was in the grip of a building panic attack.

Lulu heard herself say, 'I have no intention of going anywhere.'

He straightened up, and for a long, awful moment Lulu thought he was going to turn around and leave her here.

Please don't abandon me.

The words were forced up from deep inside her, where a small frightened girl was still cowering.

Then she realised he was walking away, and an awful

cold feeling began to invade her limbs, only for him to stop at the front of the car.

'Pop the hood,' he called to her.

Lulu scrambled to obey him, jamming her middle with the gearstick but hardly noticing. He would never know how grateful she was that he wasn't going anywhere, and she knew she was safe as long as she stayed in the car.

All she needed now was to keep her adrenal glands from overshooting the mark.

She fumbled in her bag for her handkerchief, soaked in lavender, peppermint and rosemary oil, and held it to her nose with one hand as she attached the earbuds to her mp3 player and pushed them into her ears with the other.

She shut her eyes and willed the meditation track she'd been listening to throughout the flight to drop her back into her own little world, where nothing could harm her.

Alejandro checked the connections and then opened the back door to grab a hand towel from the storage space under the front seat.

The little French princess was plugged into her music, a handkerchief at her nose to block out the odour of the sheep...the farmer...of anything that offended her delicate sensibilities. Which probably included him.

There's a name for men who force themselves on unwilling women.

Bull.

He shut the rear door with a slam.

Lulu pulled the earbuds out and looked around with a start. She transferred her attention to the raised bonnet.

Which was when it occurred to her that he was at the wrong end of the car.

The sheep appeared to have moved on. Carefully she edged open the door and, when it felt safe, stepped out onto the road. Nothing happened. The ground didn't tilt under her, and there was nothing but the smell of fresh grass and sheep manure and peat. She inhaled. It wasn't bad.

Alejandro saw the flash of turquoise skirts disappear to the rear of the car. The boot came up.

He lowered the bonnet and came around to find Lulu wrestling the spare tyre out of the wheel well.

'Should I ask what you're doing?'

She ignored him, yanking at the tyre with both hands, moving it to the rim of the boot and then bouncing it onto the ground.

With a little lift of her chin she rolled it around to lean it against the side of the car.

'I suppose a better question is do you *know* what you're doing?' he asked, his voice taking on a note of real amusement.

In answer, she retrieved the canvas bag tucked to the side of the wheel well, untied it and produced the wheel brace like a trophy, together with the jack and jack handle, which she laid out on the ground.

Alejandro gave her a grudging nod of respect and Lulu felt a small surge of confidence.

There was very little she had to thank her deadbeat dad for, but the fact that she could change a tyre, fix a leaky tap and unclog the drains in a bathroom were all down to a childhood when she hadn't had a choice. Maman hadn't been able to afford help—they'd had to do everything themselves.

'You might want to take those shoes off first, *querida*,' he suggested.

She gave that the disdainful look that comment deserved. 'I'm an ex-ballerina. After *pointes* four-inch heels are nothing.'

Still, it was a bit of a wrestle to get the hubcap off and keep her balance, so he might have had a point, but once she had it free she used the wheel brace to loosen the nuts. She crouched down in a puff of satin and tulle underskirts and positioned the jack under the car.

She was aware that Alejandro was leaning over her for a

closer look. Determined to do a good job, she began turning the jack handle and the car lifted with a slow creak.

When the wheel was clear of the ground she clasped it on either side and pulled.

The weight of it had her staggering backwards, and she gave an *'ouf'* as Alejandro caught and steadied her.

Lulu had the oddest sensation that she would have liked to stay there, with his big solid body sheltering her and his hands sending all sorts of messages to parts of her she had grown used to ignoring.

'That's enough,' he said in his deep voice. 'I'll finish this.'

For a moment Lulu had an altogether different image in her mind from the one she beheld as he let her go, stepped in and lifted the spare tyre with enviable ease, swiftly replacing all the wheel nuts with the brace and winding the jack in a reverse position to lower the car to the ground.

He's turned me into a nymphomaniac, she thought. Who knew what he did to women who already liked sex?

He tightened the nuts and shoved the hubcap back into place, replaced the old wheel in the boot, along with the tools, and slammed down the lid.

Lulu had her hand out.

'Give me the keys,' she said.

Alejandro knew where this was going, but it was no skin off his nose. He handed them over.

She marched around to the driver's seat, casting him a pointed look over the roof of the car. 'Well, get in.'

He grinned and eased his muscled frame in beside her.

Violets. The scent was hot in his nostrils now. They flared appreciably.

She didn't look like the girl he'd picked up this morning. Her dark curls were ruffled in a halo around a face that was reddened either from the wind or exertion or just sheer temper. Her dark eyes shone and her skirt was sadly crumpled. There was a grease stain on her top. But, with her jacket neatly folded on the back seat, she was showing off two neat little scoops of bosom above the tight neckline of her top.

He noticed that her shoes, now caked in mud, had been discarded in the passenger footwell and she had a look of fierce concentration on her face.

She looked exactly the way she had when he'd kissed her, wild and beautiful, and it sharpened his hunger for her.

She pulled out onto the road and took off.

'You might want to watch your speed,' he observed, unable to take his eyes off her.

'You might want to tell me why you thought it was fine to leave me locked in a car in the middle of nowhere.'

'You weren't locked in, and I went to find out what we needed to know.' He eyed her stained clothing. 'What I can't work out is why you put on that little show back there about not getting out of the car—'

'None of your business.'

'When you're so clearly capable.'

She glanced at him, a little dumbfounded, then looked back at the road. He was glad she was concentrating on the road.

'Yes, I am. Capable.'

'Do you know where we're going, *querida*?'

She changed gear and pushed those wild curls out of her eyes in a defiant gesture. 'Of course I do.'

He noted the sign to Inverary as it flashed past. His gaze dropped to those twin scoops, rising and falling gently above her neckline, to the sensual pout of her lower lip above that jaunty little chin.

She looked so pleased with herself he decided not to inform her that they were going the wrong way. He was in no hurry to get to the castle, to be bored to death by talk of for ever and happy-ever-after. No... He settled back comfortably, folded his arms across his chest and pretended to close his eyes. He was going to let this run a little longer, and then, when she'd run out of steam and learned her lesson, he'd think about taking this chemistry between them to its natural conclusion.

Lulu peered out at the passing countryside. According to her map, shouldn't they be approaching the motorway by now? It was growing dark, and it was raining, and she didn't have a clue where they were.

The ribbon of road had grown narrower and it was impossible to read the signs. The headlights on the car lit up only the road ahead, making everything that lay outside it seem menacing and vaguely supernatural.

Lulu liked the countryside—in the daylight, and from the confines of a car, and preferably not stopping. But she was going to have to pull over. The fuel tank was bobbing close to empty.

She brought the car to a stop on the shoulder of the road. Then reached over and touched Alejandro's impressive shoulder.

He felt warm and reassuringly powerful beneath her hand.

He didn't stir.

She gave him a more definite push. 'Mr du Crozier.'

No response.

'Alejandro!'

Thick sable lashes lifted and his eyes gleamed speculatively over her in the same way the headlights lit up the road ahead. He was looking at her as if she were naked, which was disconcerting enough, and Lulu had a sudden, completely outrageous thought that he hadn't been sleeping at all.

'We appear to be lost,' she said unwillingly.

'You don't say?'

His voice was husky, but not with sleep. Lulu swallowed. There was something very intimate about their proximity, as if the darkness outside and the quiet within had made the space between them somehow more personal.

Lulu licked her lips. 'I don't know where we are.'

'Fortunate, isn't it,' he said in that low, taunting voice, 'that I do?'

He undid his seatbelt and opened the car door.

'*I'm* driving,' he said unnecessarily.

Lulu released the breath she hadn't known she was holding and, rather than stepping outside, scrambled nimbly over the gearbox and tucked her skirts around her in the passenger seat.

Alejandro took the wheel and swung the car back out onto the road.

'How do you know?' she demanded.

'I saw the last sign. We're just outside Inverness.'

Relief swamped her. Then she frowned. 'But you were asleep.'

'Let's just say I'm not a heavy sleeper, *querida*,' he responded with a glint in his eyes.

She knew it! Impossible man. But her heart was pounding a little, and she found herself watching him and waiting to see what he'd do next.

Alejandro had them on the motorway within ten short minutes. Lulu discovered she was feeling a little out of sorts now her adventure was over.

She tried to envisage the weekend ahead on her own, and it was so depressing that in her head she found herself shaping sentences she didn't know if she had the guts to go through with, let alone ask.

I'm on my own this weekend...you're on your own. I'm maid of honour...you're best man. Doesn't it make sense if we pair up? Maybe you could kiss me again?

And that was when a huge gust of wind buffeted the car and all the available light left in the sky dwindled to nothing and the rain came down.

Alejandro slowed them to a crawl, along with the two or three other vehicles on the road.

'Kilantree…' she read from the sign ahead under the spray of their headlights. 'One mile. Is Kilantree near Dunlosie Castle?' she asked.

'Not near enough.'

To her surprise, Alejandro eased the car into the turn-off lane.

'What are you doing?'

'It's dark, it's raining, and I don't know these roads. We won't make Dunlosie tonight.'

'What does that mean?'

Although all of a sudden she *did* know, and for the first time in years having her routine destroyed didn't bring on feelings of anxiety. Quite the contrary…

'We're spending the night here.'

CHAPTER SIX

THE DIRECTIONS THEY'D received at the pub in Kilantree's main street took them just out of town and up a long steep drive to Mrs Bailey's B&B. The place proved to be a fairly substantial cottage. The eponymous Mrs Bailey appeared in dressing gown and slippers.

'Well, now, bring the lassie in—you'll be blown away out there. How are you, m'dear? You look pale as a ghost! We've got one of those, but I'm sure it won't bother you tonight.'

'Ghost?'

Lulu's eyes sought his. She didn't look amused.

Alejandro was aware that her small hand had slipped into his.

'It brings the tourists in, no doubt?' he commented, and Mrs Bailey laughed.

'Aye, it does—but that's not to say it doesn't exist. Come up these stairs. You don't mind carrying your own luggage, do you? My husband is already in bed. He has a four a.m. start with the sheep.'

Lulu's expression said, *More sheep?*

Alejandro suppressed a smile. He had to duck at the top of the stairs. The ceilings were low and age permeated the very beams of the place.

The older woman opened a door on a bedroom so snug the double bed itself and a chest of drawers took up most of the room.

There was an unlit fireplace that their landlady began fussing with.

'We'll have you warm in no time. I'll bring ye up some dinner in a half-hour, if that suits. The bathroom is at the end of the hall and there are fresh towels.'

Lulu's mouth had fallen open. 'I am *not* sharing this room with you,' she hissed as Mrs Bailey closed the door.

He was ready for this. 'It's fine, *querida*, I trust you.'

She rolled her eyes, but he noticed her gaze was expectant. He wasn't going to be making the first move this time. He needed this to be very clearly *her* decision.

'You should have explained the situation to her.'

He folded his arms.

'There's only one bed!'

'*Sí*, it looks comfortable.'

It was her turn to fold her arms.

'I'm afraid you'll have to sleep on the floor,' she said.

They both looked at the stretch of floorboards between them.

'No,' he said.

She flushed.

'Maybe you can sleep in the chair,' she suggested, as if she was being helpful.

He raised an eyebrow. 'How about we toss a coin for it?'

She opened her mouth, and then at the expression on his face shut it.

He pulled a coin from his back pocket. 'Heads or tails?'

'Heads.'

He flipped the coin, slid his hand away. 'Tails. I'll give you a blanket.'

He could feel her eyes boring into him as he set about improving Mrs Bailey's attempt at a fire. He was half minded just to scoop her off her feet and put her mind at rest. He had no intention of sleeping alone.

'I need my things,' she said, her voice a little loud given he was right there.

He shoved one of the logs deeper into the smouldering ash.

'Are you going to do the right thing or make me go outside again?'

'I'll be a gentleman,' he said, straightening up to find her watching him owlishly, 'and get them.'

She backed up as he headed out. Timid as a dormouse.

'The little blue case will be enough,' she called after him when he was halfway down the hall. 'And don't shake it about.'

Alejandro was coming inside with the blue case he wasn't supposed to shake when he met Mrs Bailey at the bottom of the stairs.

'I'll include a bottle of brandy with your dinner, laddie. Your wife looks like she needs a little warming up.'

Alejandro nodded a brief thanks, but knew the only thing warming up Lulu would be him.

If he'd been a less confident man he might have taken pause when Lulu met him at the top of the stairs, uttered an unconvincing *'Merci beaucoup,'* snatched her suitcase and, with a suspicious look at him, as if he were a villainous seducer, fled for the bathroom at the end of the hall, slamming the door.

But confidence had never been his problem, and Alejandro grinned and went back downstairs to find out about their meal.

When he returned, carrying a wooden tray, Lulu was rummaging around in her suitcase. She looked up, her big brown eyes doing that uncertain thing again, but that was before she noticed the bottle under his arm and the two glasses wedged between his blunt fingers.

She leapt to her feet. 'That's my wedding crystal!'

'Sí.' He shrugged. 'We'll rinse them and they'll never know.'

'I'll know!'

'We can eat on the floor,' he said, ignoring her outburst, and settled the tray on the hearth. Then he took a better look at her new outfit. It was wool, full-length, and buttoned up to her neck. 'Whose grandmother did you steal that from?'

Lulu's face fell as she glanced down at her dressing gown. 'I heard that the Scottish nights are cold because of the North Sea,' she said seriously.

'The North Sea?'

'Out there.' She waved her hand vaguely at the wall.

By Alejandro's calculations she was pointing inland, or at a stretch of the Atlantic.

He didn't like her dressing gown, Lulu thought, tugging uneasily at the sleeves. But it was practical, and that was what mattered.

Lulu noticed his hair was wet from the rain, and that he'd brought the scent of the wild outdoors in on his clothes. Her senses stirred. More than stirred. He'd braved the elements for her. She shouldn't find that sexy...but she did. Her gaze went a little helplessly to the stretch of damp fabric across his upper body, the swell of muscle, the hard male bones.

'Are you going to eat?'

Lulu realised she'd just been standing there all this time, and that he'd caught her checking him out.

Flustered, she made a production of sitting down on the rug and surveying their dinner. It was stew and dumplings. The kind of food she would have been careful around if she hadn't been on a break.

'What's that?' she asked rather desperately as he uncorked the bottle.

'It's one of the bottles of burgundy I brought over for Khaled and Gigi. They won't miss one.'

Lulu held out her hand and examined the old faded label. '1945?' she said.

'It was produced at the end of World War II—I sourced a handful of bottles through Christie's.'

'You bought wine at an *auction*?'

'Why not?'

'Wasn't it a little expensive?'

He angled a speculative look her way that set all the hormones in her body aquiver. 'Just a little.'

'This feels so wasteful,' Lulu half whispered as she watched him expertly decant the blood-dark wine into goblets. 'I'm sure Mrs Bailey's stew isn't up to the standards of a forty-five burgundy.'

'Good wine improves everything,' he told her, and she knew he wasn't talking about the wine.

She found herself checking to see that none of her buttons had come undone.

Non, all accounted for. To settle her nerves Lulu concentrated on sipping her wine. It slid down like heaven, and she gave a soft sigh of approval and looked over at him— only to discover he hadn't touched his. He was watching her, and she was instantly back in the car with him, his hand at the back of her head, his mouth making all kinds of magic with hers, leaving her breathless and flustered all over again.

'So,' he said with intent, 'from ballerina to topless showgirl. How did you get there?'

Lulu glared at him. Sprawled against the post at the end of the bed, long powerful legs stretched out across the rug, bare feet idling in the firelight, he looked like every fantasy any woman could ever have. And he knew it.

Not hers, though. She wanted Gregory Peck. She wanted someone decent and reliable who would always give up his bed to a lady and would not expect her to share it—and he certainly wouldn't make assumptions about her profession.

Although she guessed half the dancers at L'Oiseau Bleu *were* topless—*nude*—there wasn't anything wrong with that; it was artistic. There was a whole heritage behind it. But Alejandro probably didn't care much about the history of things. He just liked naked women.

Which shouldn't have her gaze lingering just a little too long on the wide, sensual line of his mouth. That dark shadow was already making itself known around it and along his jaw, hinting at a heavy beard. She wondered if it would scratch a little if he kissed her again...

Lulu fanned herself. 'The fire is very warm.'

'You'll be glad of it later tonight, when the temperature plummets,' he commented.

She glanced at the bed and then met his eyes. She waited for him to volunteer to take the chair. He didn't.

Tightening her lips, she reached for her glass of wine.

'So, from completely rude man to professional polo player. How did that happen?'

He didn't even flinch. 'I was put on a horse when I was four years old and my father handed me a mallet, I didn't have much choice.'

Against her will, Lulu's sympathies were stirred. She tried to picture him at four. She failed. He was so big and testosterone-fuelled it was hard to imagine him small and vulnerable.

'Even if I hadn't been, my family has bred horses in Argentina for many generations and the sport is popular in my country. It's in the blood.'

'So you inherited everything?' she said, still annoyed about the bed.

If he behaved like a gentleman she might—*might*—consider sharing it with him. Platonically.

Although Alejandro du Crozier did not strike her as the platonic type.

He was the type to grab a woman and kiss her until she slapped him and then leave her to the mercy of a hundred black-faced sheep.

'Inherited?' He appeared to inspect the word. 'No, I earned it. Every acre, every pound of horse flesh, every match. No hand-outs,' he said, with an emphasis that made her think she'd hit a nerve. He paused, taking a mouthful of wine. 'I run a working *estancia*, Lulu,' he added, meeting her eyes, 'and I have a corporate portfolio that among other things supports our national polo team.'

'That must keep you busy.'

'You have no idea, *querida*.'

No, but she was going to. Once she started college in a month's time, coupled with a full season at L'Oiseau Bleu. That was pretty impressive on its own, although she guessed it didn't stand up to breeding horses and captaining his country in international polo matches.

'I don't know anything about polo, but it must take a lot of work—with the horses, I mean.'

'You get out of it what you put in. But, *sí*, it's all about the ponies. You're only as competitive as your mount.'

She imagined *he* was incredibly competitive. You didn't get to that level in a professional sport without it.

Weirdly, she liked it. She liked his assurance…the way he got things done. Mostly she liked talking like this with him.

For the first time it occurred to her that maybe she could have tonight for herself. The other girls weren't here to tell him that there was something wrong with her…her parents weren't here to make it abundantly clear that there was something wrong with her. She didn't even have any responsibilities to Gigi tonight.

This could be *her* night. Which meant she had to stop talking on and on about polo!

She took a big gulp of wine. 'Your parents must be proud of you.'

Alejandro shifted his long legs in front of the fire restlessly.

'They divorced when I was fifteen,' he said easily.

He was a child of divorced parents, just like her. They had something in common.

'I didn't have much to do with my father after that,' he added, swirling the contents of his glass.

'Divorce can be tough.'

He raised a sceptical eyebrow. 'My parents conducted a war of attrition, Lulu. Divorce was the day peace was declared.'

She knew exactly what he meant. But she wasn't opening up that can of worms. 'Did you stay with your mother?'

'*Sí*, we stayed with her—my sisters and I.' He took another mouthful of wine and then put down the glass. 'Before you ask, *querida*, my mother is too busy with her new husband in Rio de Janeiro to follow my career now.'

Ouch. But he looked too big and tough to really care.

'So your father put you on a horse—but why did you choose to play professionally once you grew up? You must enjoy it.'

'I'm naturally competitive.' He said it the same way someone might say their eye colour was brown. 'I've had the opportunity to play against the world's best. Why pass it up?'

He made it sound so easy. Lulu wondered what he'd say if he knew that some days she couldn't even go outside.

'I admit polo takes up a lot of the time I'd prefer to spend on the ranch, but I think it's worth it if my involvement helps popularise the sport. My ex-wife would probably disagree. Professional sport takes its toll on your personal life.'

'You've been married?'

'This surprises you?'

'It's just you don't look like the marrying kind.'

He cast a speculative look her way. 'What kind *do* I look like?'

'Busy,' she said, a little astonished by her own boldness.

'Not as busy as you imagine, *querida*,' he drawled, with a faint hint of a smile, and Lulu suddenly couldn't hear above the thundering of her pulse.

She hadn't done the prep for this. Being interested in a man, flirting, and all the while wondering what he really thought of her.

Not much, she suspected.

'We have an internationally renowned breeding programme on the *estancia*,' he went on.

Just when she thought she had the measure of him he got more impressive.

'It's how I got to know Khaled—sourcing Kabardian stock in the Caucasus a few years ago. We got tight.'

Lulu didn't want to talk about Khaled Kitaev. But she realised she'd stumbled into something she'd heard about from the other girls at the cabaret. *Talk to a man about what fascinates him and he'll think you're riveting.*

'So you're the best friend,' he said, immediately confounding her expectation that he would only want to talk about himself.

'Pardon?'

'Of Gigi. You were flatmates? Was that the set-up?'

Disconcerted that he knew that much about her, Lulu wondered a little uneasily what else Khaled and Gigi had told him. *Nothing*, she decided. *They would have told him nothing.*

'We auditioned for the Bluebirds at the same time,' she explained self-consciously, 'and Gigi was looking for a flat. My parents had arranged one for me in a nice neighbourhood, so she moved in.'

She glanced up at his dry chuckle.

'What is so funny? You think my parents shouldn't help pay my rent? Didn't *your* parents help you out when you got started in life?'

'My parents just got in the way, frankly, *querida*, and no, they didn't. Relax—I'm not judging.'

Lulu narrowed her eyes on the faint amusement that danced around his wide, disturbingly sensual mouth.

He *was* judging.

She wondered what he'd say if he knew that in addition to living in her beautiful flat, owned by her parents, she was driven everywhere by her mother or her stepfather's driver, and her bills were often met by her parents. It was all part of the highly stratified life put in place for her when she was eighteen, to cushion her anxieties. What would he think of her if he knew she was a walking, talking failure at the game of life?

'So it's just you in the parents-endorsed flat nowadays?'

'Yes,' she said slowly, not sure where this was going.

'Is this why you resent him?'

'Who?'

'Khaled. Gigi's done well for herself.'

A cold feeling pooled in Lulu's belly and a hot feeling flashed up through her. What did he mean? What was he implying?

'I do not resent him. Who told you that? I'm very happy for Gigi.' She was aware she had raised her voice. She never raised her voice. 'And what do you mean, she's done well for herself?'

'He's writing her some pretty big cheques.'

Lulu almost choked. 'Excuse me? Gigi is not marrying Khaled for his *money*!'

'I'm aware of that. I was talking about you.'

'Me?' she spluttered. 'I don't want Khaled's money!' She sucked in a breath. 'Do you mean am I looking for a billionaire of my own?'

'You wouldn't be the first girl.'

CHAPTER SEVEN

THE WEALTH OF cynicism in that comment left Lulu flabbergasted.

'Gigi and I weren't starring in our own version of *How to Marry a Millionaire*, if that's what you mean,' she said, trying to sound as dismissive as he did, but knowing it just came out defensively. 'We're working girls. Gigi's still working. She runs the cabaret. I *work*!'

'You're a woman who by her own admission is supported by her parents.'

Lulu went to deny it, but she couldn't, and nor could she explain her circumstances. It was so frustrating!

'You wouldn't be the first person to want what your friend's got. Maybe I'm wrong...' He shrugged.

Lulu hated him for that shrug, as if it didn't matter one way or the other. It *did* matter when you were the one being unjustly accused!

'You *are* wrong! And Khaled Kitaev has no right to talk about me to you or anyone.'

'He's hardly said a word.' Alejandro leaned back, all wide shoulders and amused speculation. 'I'd worked you out five minutes into that flight, *querida*.'

'You'd *worked me out*?' Lulu could feel herself crumbling inside like a sandcastle.

'Troublemaker.'

'What...?' The word emerged as a whisper.

All of a sudden she was convinced he knew everything about her. Gigi might not have spilled her secrets to Khaled, but somehow this man knew everything.

Did he know she'd never had a boyfriend? Probably. Did he think she was some kind of misfit freak? Probably.

Did he think it was funny, making a joke of spending the night with her?

Her confidence hit an all-time low.

Khaled had taken her best friend away and it had felt as if a large piece of her inhabited land had been annexed by a ruthless invading force because her private world was already so small. How would Alejandro like it if he was forced to question everything about his life, let alone try to start again?

But she couldn't begin to explain it to this man.

And why should she?

'What have I done to make you say those things to me?' she defended herself. 'All you've done is attack me since we met on the plane. I'm not a bad person, but I think you want me to be awful so you can take your bad mood out on me. I thought—I thought when you kissed me—'

Mon Dieu, what was she saying? Lulu scrambled to her feet, belatedly aware that there wasn't anywhere to go.

Her *derrière* hit the bed-end.

'You don't know a thing about me,' she muttered fiercely, turning her back on him, 'and I hope after this weekend we never see each other again.'

Alejandro's first instinct was to turn her in his arms and kiss her. But the last time he'd done that she'd been upset, and he'd just had his conscience slammed up against the wall.

He dated independent, self-assured women every time. Not that it always worked out. His ex-wife had independently propelled herself into other men's beds. But Lulu's words had truth to them.

Everything about her rang true.

Was he still judging other women by his relationship with his ex-wife?

Sometimes it was just about chemistry and timing. Both of which he had here. He was wasting it by twisting this girl around the knot that had been his long-ago short-lived marriage.

He looked at her rigid shoulders and it occurred to him that this was about her only defence with him.

She'd been using it all day.

He felt even more like a bully.

'Forgive me, Lulu, it's been a long day and I've unfairly taken it out on you.'

Lulu hadn't expected an apology, and she hadn't expected him to be on his feet so fast and standing behind her. She didn't want to turn around because she knew her face would be red and her mascara streaky.

More, she didn't want to turn around because she suddenly felt at a loss as to what was expected of her, and she wasn't quite sure what this tension between them was.

'Lulu?'

'I accept your apology,' she said stiffly.

There was an odd little silence, in which Lulu suffered the indignity of knowing he probably just felt sorry for her. Which was about as sexy as porridge.

'We could try to just be civil to one another, do you think?' she said in a small voice.

'Agreed. But I'm finding being civil to you taxing.'

'Why?' She looked up over her shoulder at him.

Why was he looking at her like that? He could probably hear her heart beating. Beating? It was fairly stomping, like the chorus at L'Oiseau Bleu when they were still learning new moves.

'I think you know why.' There was a faint smile on his lips but those eyes were serious, and they promised things she couldn't quite get a clear visual on. She knew only that they would probably put what they'd done in the car into the shade.

It was the unknown, and Lulu knew she was losing traction on all her firmly held beliefs about herself as she began the slide towards it. A little too fast for her...a little too soon. But everything seemed to go fast when she was around this man.

One minute she truly hated him, and the fact that he'd seen her at her most foolish made it worse.

But now she was tempted beyond belief just to step up to him, pull at his shirt and make him kiss her again.

But that wasn't going to happen now.

'I really think I should go to bed,' she said, and told herself she wasn't disappointed when he didn't argue with her.

Alejandro returned from the bathroom freshly shaven, dressed in boxer shorts and with bare feet, to find Lulu in the armchair.

He'd assumed she'd take the bed as her due. Obviously not. Her expression in the lamplight was serious, and there was something about the way she was evidently trying to find a way to make herself comfortable that he recognised in other things she'd done today. It was crazy, but he got the idea she was trying her hardest.

Alejandro looked at the bed, and then at the girl curling herself up in the chair.

Dios.

Deep down he'd known from the start that he'd have to take the chair. She'd never been going to share that bed with him.

She would sleep in the bed and he'd play footman in her fairytale, try to arrange his large frame on that armchair and get what shut-eye he could.

He'd slept in the saddle before.

He could manage a badly sprung armchair in a Scottish farmhouse.

He dumped his toiletries bag, strode over and scooped her up, blanket and all. It was a mistake, because everything suddenly felt incredibly intimate between them. The lovely weight of her, his arms around her... She felt like *his.*

She seemed to know it, because she didn't struggle.

He put her on the bed.

'What are you doing?'

'What does it look like? I'm giving you the bed.'

That was when he realised she'd shed the dressing gown. The blanket was pooled at her hips and Lulu was sitting up in the sexiest lingerie ensemble he'd ever seen.

Or maybe it was just the girl wearing it.

Some kind of vintage cream satin bra and panties trimmed in old-fashioned white lace. Later, when he was thinking with his brain again, he would wonder what it was about that white lace...

But now he was more interested in the soft pale curves poured into it.

She was delicate, and more lovely than anything he'd ever seen.

She'd also seen him. The snug boxers didn't hide much.

She looked fascinated, and it was only when the mattress gave under his weight and he got close enough to feel the warmth of her body that she seemed to realise she was only wearing her underwear. She made a wordless gesture, pulling the blanket towards her, which should have stopped him. He kissed her anyway. But not as he had kissed her in the car, with his blood up and her mouth full of snippy demands and his male ego making him want to prove a point.

His blood was up, all right, but he was looking to prove something else.

That he was good enough for her.

That she could trust him.

That she was *his*.

Tomorrow he would have to share her with everyone at the wedding, but right now she was his, and he realised that this knowledge had been growing from the moment he'd boarded that flight and set eyes on her—before everything else had intervened between them.

She pulled away first, looking at him as if she was every bit as stunned by this turn of events as he was.

'I don't know—' she began, and it was everything he didn't want to hear.

He watched her, waiting.

Lulu could see his amber eyes gleaming beneath those ridiculously long, thick sable lashes, holding all kinds of knowledge she wanted to have. He was one of the most beautiful men she'd ever seen. He made her feel so...*alive*, and he hadn't treated her like glass all day. He'd been absolutely, appallingly awful to her. Just the thought made her body ache a little more for him.

If I don't have sex with him I'll regret it for the rest of my life.

Even before she could think about doing it she was tracing the seam of his parted lips with her fingertip.

He took her hand and gently folded her fingers into a fist. 'You are not sure, *hermosa*.'

'I am.'

'I'm not looking for a relationship, and I think you are.'

Lulu weighed that up. *Non*, she knew how hard relationships were to sustain when you were trapped in your own fears, as she was. She knew she couldn't have that.

'That's not what I want.'

'No?'

Frankly, she didn't know what she wanted—other than what she was having right now. When what she'd been having for far too many years was—nothing.

'I just want something different,' she admitted.

'Different from what?'

Where did she begin? Lulu tried to find words that just wouldn't come. Everything was bound up so tightly inside her—safe and sound, she'd once thought. But she was beginning to feel like a prisoner, locked up along with her anxieties.

Alejandro watched the struggle on her face. She couldn't answer him because he suspected 'different' for her was having sex outside a relationship.

He *always* had sex outside relationships, and there was the salient difference between them.

This was going to kill him.

'You've had an exciting day, a little wine, and you don't know what you want. I don't want to be the man who takes advantage of that.'

As he spoke Lulu found herself being boxed very neatly back into the corner she'd fought so hard to get out of.

Poor invalid Lulu, whose disability always had to be taken into account.

In this case that disability appeared to be her inexperience with men.

'You'll regret this in the morning,' he assured her, as if he knew best. 'And I don't do regrets.'

She remembered what he'd told her about his parents. A war of attrition.

Her parents hadn't been at war—her mother had been a civilian casualty, with her biological father rampaging about like a one-man vigilante mob, until the day Félicienne had got up the courage to leave.

But being brave was something Lulu recognised she'd lost touch with. Somehow she'd allowed her courage to slip away, with the tide of her childhood going out and the sea of her anxieties rushing in.

Seeing the risk to her friendship with Gigi had been the catalyst to make her want to change all that.

It had taken something that big to push her out into the open.

Because of that determination to change she was sitting on this bed tonight, in the middle of the Scottish countryside, with a gorgeous, fascinating man—and he was the man she wanted.

She wasn't just someone he could put in a box labelled *'Defective'*.

He thought she'd be like glue. Sticking to him all weekend because she was so needy.

Well, she was. Needy, that was. Her whole body felt as if it had been stirred up by his kisses and there was an ache low in her pelvis. And although she knew it would go away, and also knew she would eventually fall asleep, when tomorrow came she would have lost her chance to know what it felt like to have this intimate connection with another person.

It was entirely probable, given the circumstances of her life and her condition that she was going to never have this chance again.

I don't do regrets.

Well, neither did she. Before she could chicken out Lulu rose up on her knees. In a single move she wrapped her long legs around him and looked at him fiercely.

Any arguments Alejandro had against this fell away.

He was a man, not a monk. And Lulu was… She was…

Lowering herself onto his lap, draping her slender arms over his shoulders.

'I don't want anything more than tonight,' she said, and Alejandro found himself at her mercy as her eyes dusted over the top of his bare chest as if mesmerised by him. 'Just one night—with you.'

She fitted her mouth to his inexpertly and want shuddered through his body.

He caught her face in his hands, because in a moment there wouldn't be any going back.

'Are you sure?' he made himself ask.

She smiled, a dimple winking alongside her mouth as she bent to kiss him again.

He took over then. His tongue made forays along her lower lip, into her mouth, and Lulu could feel the fire burning inside her. He was stoking it with his mouth.

Not just his mouth.

Lulu could feel him against her most intimate place, much bigger than she'd ever imagined, and hard, and his hands on her satin-covered bottom were bringing her into closer contact.

Lulu couldn't believe how aroused she was getting, or how much she wanted him. His shoulders felt like rock under her hands, but his flesh was hot and springy. He felt so alive, and for the first time she began to understand the scale of what she'd been missing. She'd only been half alive, and that didn't have much to do with sex, although that was a part of it. It was just that the fear had taken so much away from her and she'd let it.

She wasn't letting this go.

She was having this.

It was hers.

He broke their kiss to give her one last warning, 'I'm not looking for anything more than this, Lulu.'

'Bon,' she said breathlessly, ignoring everything but what she was finding with him.

Alejandro slid his hand under the satin and lace bra and found skin much softer than the satin that had encased it, and an astonishingly plump breast for such a slight girl, with a taut little nipple that seemed to furl under his touch.

Madre di Dios.

He rubbed, she whimpered, and he said a word of prayer under his breath, because this was pushing him to the brink and he hadn't even got her naked.

She was breathing in low, shallow pants that were growing more frantic. He could deal with that. He took one taut lace-covered nipple gently between his teeth and sucked. She gave an almost startled cry before he applied the same attention to the other, sliding his hand under the loose leg of her cami-knickers. She felt so soft and wet and warm and he couldn't wait.

He shoved down his boxers.

She knelt on the bed, just looking, her eyes all over him and her expression almost unbearable in its curiosity.

Then she seemed to remember herself, and reached

around to unhook her bra. But he was there before her. He could feel the subtle tension in her body as he carefully peeled down the straps and she held out her arms to let the satin and lace drop away. Her breasts were crested with raspberry-coloured nipples. She actually raised her arms again to cover herself—an act of modesty he recognised but one that didn't make sense. He witnessed a flash of uncertainty in the eyes she lifted to his, but then she set her chin and slowly took her arms away.

Alejandro was convinced he saw that chin jut out a little more.

A tenderness spread through him that somehow wasn't at odds with the lust tearing at his insides.

He ran his hands gently over her shoulders, down her arms, watching the tightening of the buds of her nipples, the way her breasts lifted slightly with the deep shuddering breath she took. She put the palms of her hands to his shoulders, ran them over his arms in a mimicking movement.

'Are we going to have sex?'

It was a crazy question, but it was one he took seriously because it was Lulu asking.

'Only if you want to.'

'Mmm. Yes. I want to.' She put her arms around his neck as he came over her. 'With *you*,' she said, looking into his eyes.

He considered asking who else? There was nobody but them in the room. But her words reminded him of how sweet she was.

Sweet and sexy and not like any other woman he'd ever been with.

'Lulu?'

'Mmm?'

'Just tonight.'

'Stop saying that.' She screwed up her nose.

She was right. This wasn't about her—it was *him*. He

was finding an intensity in this experience and as a man of experience it gave him pause.

But not enough to stop. He couldn't have stopped now if the whole damn farmhouse had collapsed around them.

Besides, she'd assured him she only wanted one night. It was his problem if it felt like something more.

He put his hands to her cami-knickers and drew them down, past her ankles, feasting his eyes on her.

She had surprisingly rounded hips, and tiny dark curls at the apex of her thighs, and her skin had clearly never seen the sun—it was like snow.

Lulu was breathing shallowly. There was something touchingly private about the way she watched him, as if trying to work out what he was thinking.

He could have told her what he was thinking—that he was the luckiest man in Scotland tonight.

Her eyes were big, her mouth wet from their kisses. Her nipples looked like bright jewels against her flushed breasts.

Her arms tightened around his neck.

'I have to tell you something,' she blurted out.

'Tell me.' He tried not to sound too gruff, because right now talking wasn't high on his agenda.

'I watch a lot of old films.'

Alejandro looked at her and wondered if lust could jam up your hearing.

'You watch old films?' he repeated huskily.

She nodded. 'There's a film… Joanne Woodward…Paul Newman. It's very good.' She moistened her lips. 'It's about a girl who tried love once but it didn't stick. So she's given up on men.'

'Good. I'll watch it some time.'

He lowered his mouth to her throat, where the skin was soft as satin. But Lulu kept talking.

'She's a semi-maiden.'

His head came up. He looked into her eyes, surprise registering. 'This is you?'

She nodded, no longer talking, just fixing those big brown eyes on him.

He wasn't completely taken off guard, but there was something about her admitting it and giving him that trustful look that made him feel incredibly protective of her.

It's a gift, he thought. *She's giving you a gift. Her trust.*

It twisted inside him painfully. Because what did he have to give her in return? Cynicism born of a deep understanding. Most people had strings attached to gifts—everyone had a motive. Nothing was ever as it seemed.

'It's worse than being one thing or the other—you're sort of stuck.' She spoke softly, tangling her fingers in the soft whorls of dark hair on his chest. 'I'm so very, very tired of being stuck, Alejandro.'

This he could understand. She wanted a little more experience—he could give it to her.

'Let's see what we can do about it, then,' he said, and slid down the bed, parted her thighs and put his mouth on her.

She gave a squeak of dismay and a husky, *'Non!'* But her body was on board and she melted under his tongue as he had known she would, until he had her twisting, panting, pinned to the mattress as he drew an orgasm from her that had her crying out into the pillow.

He considered telling her that the Baileys assumed they were married and she could yell as loud as she liked, but there was something about her restraint that was highly erotic.

He kept his mouth where she most wanted it until she subsided and then he began again, until the throbbing in his own body became unbearable and all he could concentrate on was being inside her.

He dealt with a condom and joined her on the pillow, kissed her soft, responsive mouth. She was flushed and gratifyingly dazed.

He told himself this was what he did. He worked hard, he rode like a demon, and he gave good sex. Women didn't leave his bed disappointed.

But what he was doing now wasn't a part of that. He didn't stroke a woman's hair and gaze into her eyes, a little mesmerised by the wonder he saw there as she gazed back at him, and he didn't question why he felt so good being with her.

'Are you ready?'

She nodded and kissed him and he moved carefully over her. He nudged her thighs apart with his knee and shifted between them. He was desperate to feel her around him, but as he forged forward into that soft, slick heat there wasn't a lot of room. He was big and she was small and her body wasn't giving way.

Lulu was aware of him nudging at the heart of her and she forgot to breathe. She felt so excited—she wanted this—and yet as she shifted a little and he pressed she knew it wasn't happening. Something was wrong. She froze. Frustration and humiliation joined hands and Lulu just wanted to cry. How typical of her. She couldn't even pass through this fundamental rite of passage without her body conspiring against her.

She was useless—*useless*.

'Lulu.' Alejandro steered her face with his hand so she was looking into his eyes.

'You just need to relax,' he told her, his expression making her think he must be in some degree of pain.

Relax? She didn't want to *relax*. She wanted to have sex. She'd relax when it was over. Which looked like round about now...

Oh...

She felt his index finger gently circle her little bud of nerve-endings and familiar sensation streaked through her—only it was sharper, more intense, with him lodged partway inside her. He kept up the circular motion, sipping at her lips, and Lulu soon found herself caught up in this very nice activity that was coaxing her senses towards that blissful rippling pleasure.

It was only as she softened around him and gave way, and he forged forward inside her, that she realised what he'd done. But it was only a moment's flashing thought, because his thumb continued to stroke her and her body seemed instinctively to take up the dance, drawing him into her.

He was coaxing her with husky words to wrap her legs around him, his hands remarkably gentle as he cupped her hips. It was only then that he began to move, with immense restraint, and she knew he was doing this for her. All for her. Her breath stopped in her chest at the sweetness of it.

His jaw was locked and he was studying her face with an almost unholy intensity.

'Am I hurting you?'

She shook her head.

Lulu tried to think, but all she could do was feel. She began to give herself up to the rhythm they were creating together, and as she arched against him his thrusts lengthened. She could hear herself making small sounds, until she cried out and her entire body seemed to release around him.

His rhythm quickened and he moved inside her with a fierceness he hadn't shown before, finding his own pleasure. Buried inside her, he shuddered heavily and Lulu was overcome by a sense of utter unity with him. She revelled in the sheer animal heat of their bodies wrapped around one another.

Alejandro did his best not to collapse on top of her, and when his back hit the mattress he anchored her to him. He found himself holding her—something he never did. Which was when he became aware that Lulu was hiding her face against his shoulder. He remembered the way he'd dismissed her in the car, the way she'd hidden her face as he'd said those words to her. He hadn't understood anything. He felt a blade of self-revulsion sink deep as he wondered if he'd hurt her.

'*Dulzura...*' he said, bombarded by feelings he was damn sure he didn't recognise or want. He thought he'd made it good for her.

She lifted her head, her eyes bright as stars through those silky black curls. He was a little mesmerised by them and he'd underestimated her. She didn't look unhappy at all.

'That was amazing,' she breathed. 'When can we do it again?'

CHAPTER EIGHT

LULU'S BACK HIT his forearm, between herself and the wall, and she heard something smash on the floor.

Oh, dear.

Only Alejandro was already lifting her, and with her legs locked around his waist he was filling her so absolutely all she could concentrate on was how good it felt.

She wasn't sure if a woman with as little sexual experience as she currently had should be so adventurous right off the bat, but it was hard to argue with something that felt so amazing.

Thump, thump—her shoulder nudged at the framed cross-stitch on the wall.

She whimpered, sliding her mouth against his neck as he built their pleasure.

It was all extraordinarily illuminating, if at times a little overwhelming. Nothing he did failed to bring her pleasure.

Now, as she came apart around him, her legs wound tight around his waist, the little picture fell off the wall and she didn't have it in her to care.

In the aftermath he tumbled her onto the bed and sprawled beside her, breathing heavily.

Lulu lay on her back, feeling the cool air rush over her overheated body, and wondered at this new world opening up to her.

Her body felt replete. Her heart was still pounding, but it was from excitement and exertion, not anxiety, and her mind seemed to be pumped full of happy chemicals, because all she could formulate on her face was a smile.

She turned her head and saw a look of similar satisfaction on Alejandro's face as he looked at her.

She didn't feel one bit shy.

'You must love horses,' she said.

He began to chuckle. 'Where *has* your mind gone?'

She rolled herself onto him and propped herself up on his chest, his chest hair tickling her nipples. He bent one arm behind his head the better to look at her.

'I want to know all about you,' she confessed.

Pillow talk. It wasn't something he usually did, but Alejandro found he really didn't mind.

'I'll tell you about Luna Plateada—the beautiful stallion my great-great-grandfather brought with him to Argentina in the nineteenth century.'

'Yes, please.'

'The legend goes that the bloodline of that horse is still alive in our current champion.'

'It sounds very romantic. Is it true?'

'Practical. The story enhances the price of the stock we've bred from him.'

'Still, it's a good story.'

Lulu smiled at him, all big eyes and hot, shiny cheeks. Perspiration had stuck some of her curls to her temples and cheeks. She looked as if she'd had a wild time. He stroked them back.

'Where did your great-great-grandfather come from?'

'Curiously enough—here in Scotland. His name was Alexander Crozier—he added the "du" after he became a land baron.'

'That sounds like another romantic story.'

'To tell the truth, he was most likely a swindler and a gun-for-hire. I suspect the family legend of him washing up in Buenos Aires and meeting my great-great-grandmother, being hit by a grand passion and winning her by building up a successful ranch has more to do with his ambitions. He probably fought and stole and bribed his way into a position where he could marry into one of Buenos Aires's oldest families.'

'Why do you think that?'

'Let's just say the du Croziers haven't been known for their moderation since. It had to come from somewhere, *novia.*'

'What does that mean—*"novia"*?'

'Sweetheart.'

'Oh.'

She looked adorably flushed, and the urge to stop talking and delve back into her sweet embrace had him shifting beside her.

But he knew she had to be sore, or would be sore come the morning, because he suspected she'd been a little stretchy with the truth.

He'd never been with a virgin, but he would put money on this being her first time and it made him feel responsible for her in some way—or that was as close to his feelings as he wanted to investigate.

'So when did you learn to change a tyre?' He settled back against the headboard, hooking Lulu in against him. 'You don't look like the tyre-changing type.'

'I was ten years old and we got a flat on a motorway. A man stopped and offered to show my mother how to change it. Maman isn't great with practical things, so he showed me instead.'

'Where was your father?'

Lulu had been enjoying herself, but now she felt that private part of her crouching in the corner at his question.

She opted for saying, 'He wasn't in our lives.' Which wasn't exactly the truth. Every day of her young life, even if her father had been absent, his restless, angry presence had always been felt.

'My grandfather was the one who taught me everything I needed to know,' Alejandro shared, and she got the impression he was backing off.

She relaxed against him. She didn't want to think about what was going to separate them in the morning, and besides, she was used to the idea of not involving other people in her problems.

'My father wasn't around much either—before or after the divorce,' Alejandro mused. 'And when he was it was like being hit by a cyclone of presents and energy. He would make a fuss of the girls and drag me out on some wild excursion that usually ended in someone getting hurt.'

Lulu frowned and looked up. 'He *hurt* you?'

'Fernando? No, nothing like that. He just never grew up—it was always a *Boys' Own* adventure with him. Quad bikes…fast cars when I got older. He crashed everything. I was a man at sixteen. He was—well, more of a buddy than a father.'

'What did your mother think about all this?'

'As long as he paid her bills she couldn't have cared less.'

Lulu flinched at his tone, and the urge to touch him, offer comfort, was strong in her. She hadn't had a father figure until she was fourteen, but it sounded as if Alejandro hadn't had either parent. She was so close to her own mother—perhaps too close—that it was difficult to imagine what the lack of one would feel like.

'I was the bone my parents warred with one another for. They lavished me with attention when it suited them, but when it came to the practicalities of life it was my grandfather who offered lessons.'

'But you said your father taught you to ride?'

'He put me on a saddle, smacked the horse's rump and let me fend for myself. As in riding lessons, so in life.'

He spoke without rancour, but Lulu knew enough about hiding those deepest hurts from her last year of therapy to suspect his big, tough exterior hid the boy he'd once been—longing for his father's attention and not getting it. The fact he had taken up polo professionally despite this start said a lot about his feelings for his father. She guessed it wasn't so much about wanting his father's approval as proving himself a better man.

Lulu wisely kept that observation to herself.

Alejandro ruffled the curls at her neck. He was so tactile, and she noticed he had a thing about her hair. It made her feel all squishy inside.

'Don't listen to me, *hermosa*, it's the long day talking.'

But it wasn't, and it made her feel closer to him. She watched him massage the muscle where his thigh joined his knee, stretching out his leg.

'Torn ligament a couple of months ago,' he said, following her gaze and answering her unspoken question. 'I usually patch up a lot faster than this. Must be age and fast living catching up.'

Lulu thought that if he was paying for his sins he must be like Dorian Gray—there had to be a ruined portrait somewhere—because his looks were a hymn to male beauty. He did look tired, though, and speaking about his parents had brought a seriousness into his eyes. She sensed he would not reveal any more.

She could have told him she had no intention of probing any further.

The last thing she wanted to do was rake over the coals of the long-dead bonfire that was her father's time in her life. She was too busy doing battle with spot fires—the anxieties and phobias that were its fall-out—and she knew were waiting for her tomorrow. Because they never went away.

She found her refuge in routine, and she couldn't have that this weekend.

But she was doing okay, and right now she felt better than okay. She felt something new was possible. In this room. On this night.

There hadn't been a panic attack and she knew she wouldn't have one tonight. She had never felt as safe as she did lying in his arms.

She glanced down at herself.

Lulu knew that in the real world she would feel shy,

would cover herself up, but as his gaze slid down her naked body she didn't feel anything but thrilled as his eyes darkened appreciably, and she was glad. She felt free to look at *his* body—so different from her own. He was hard where she was soft, and even her musculature after years of dance had a different, more rounded shape from the powerful planes and dips of his.

She rolled onto her side and studied the definition of his chest with her hand, gliding her fingers down over his abdomen to make sense of the ridging of muscle under the taut pull of his springy olive-toned flesh. Her hand slid down between his hairy thighs to cup him there.

Alejandro hadn't been expecting that from her. His *semi-maiden*.

He drew a breath that hissed between his teeth.

She lifted her head. 'Am I hurting you?'

'No…' he choked.

'*Bon*, I'm being as gentle as I can. I know how vulnerable men are in this area.'

He made a sound—half-snort, half-groan. 'No, you don't,' he told her. 'You don't know the half of it.'

'I was once forced to use my knee here. He hit the ground like a sack of potatoes.'

'I bet,' he grunted, before the content of what she'd just said hit him. He lifted his head. 'What do you mean, you were *forced* to?'

'I had a date who got rather pushy about where he thought the evening was going.'

Alejandro examined her face for clues as to what 'pushy' meant. 'How did he react?'

'He howled like a hyena.'

'No, I mean towards *you*.'

She bit her lip. 'After the kneeing he wasn't good for much.'

'He didn't hurt you? Physically?'

She gave an abrupt shake of her head. 'Just gave me a fright. Said some horrible things.'

Her face contorted painfully and it bothered him a great deal.

He ignored all the conditioning he'd had not to offer comfort and found himself sitting up and pulling her into the shelter of his arms. She looked both startled and pleased.

'It was over a year ago—I should be over it,' she mumbled.

'Why should you be over it?'

'I don't know. It shouldn't be that important. He said I was cold and shallow and needed to loosen up. He said—' Lulu broke off to take a deep breath. 'He said some people open a gate to life and let it in, but that I had put a lock on my gate and one day it would be old and rusty and no one would want me.'

'And you believed him?'

'No. Yes. I don't know.'

'How long had you known him?'

'Several weeks. I thought we were friends.'

She pressed her lips together and he waited, because he knew there was more.

'I don't have a lot of friends.'

It was an odd thing for her to say. He couldn't imagine she found it difficult to charm anyone. She was sweet and funny and clearly loyal, going by her friendship with Gigi.

He brushed a finger under her chin and tipped it up so he could look into her eyes. 'He wasn't your friend, Lulu. I've only known you a day and I don't see a cold, shallow person.'

'You don't really know me,' she said in a small voice.

No, he guessed he didn't, and he knew he couldn't make any false promises to her. The only way he could get to know her was to see her again—and that wasn't going to happen after this weekend. He only did weekends. Besides, they'd agreed. One night.

But why? murmured a low, persuasive voice. Why not continue over this weekend? Hell, why not fly out to the Mediterranean with her? Forget the wedding.

He could imagine Lulu's response.

It was part of the reason he was so attracted to her. Any other woman of his acquaintance would fall in with his plans without a squeak.

Lulu wouldn't just squeak—she'd give him a lecture on the duties and etiquette of being best man.

So he kissed her gently and her lips clung a little, as if she were already afraid he was going to get up out of their bed and walk away.

Nothing short of an earthquake was going to drag him away from her tonight. He already knew he wasn't going to be able to fly out on Monday and forget about her.

He also knew something else. He wanted to meet the guy who'd frightened her and knocked her confidence like this. Meet him in a back alley and take his balls off.

'I do know you're beautiful and giving, and when I'm playing in the Buenos Aires Cup next month I'm going to have a hard time concentrating on my game because I'll still be thinking about you.'

It sounded like a line, and it had begun as one, but Alejandro recognised with an odd sense of having finally found something worth having that it was also true.

She smiled at him, and while she looked pleased he could see in the flicker behind those beautiful dark eyes that she'd got the message his words were supposed to convey.

Now he just needed to convince himself.

CHAPTER NINE

THE MORNING AFTER came too soon.

Last night her fears had hidden themselves away, but Lulu was well aware that the longer she lay there in that bed in broad daylight the more easily she'd begin to make them out.

They were all coming back, like crows gathering on a wire, waiting to rush in upon her in a frenzy of flapping wings and pecking beaks.

She knew her parents were going to be waiting for her. They'd take one look at Alejandro and then her mother would take him aside and spill all.

Lulu is special. Lulu needs looking after. Are you sure you're the man for the job?

He'd take one look at the set-up and head in the other direction.

It had happened before. Julien Levolier—dance class, the summer she was almost eighteen. He'd been very keen, until the little 'talk' from her mother. At least he hadn't just hopped on his Vespa and headed off to greener pastures, where the girls were lower maintenance and able to look after themselves. No, he'd taken the time to explain first that he didn't want the hassle. She'd understood. Sort of.

She sat up and let herself appreciate Alejandro's striking physical presence as he stood fully dressed by the window, his hair damp from the shower.

He wouldn't want the hassle. Who would?

She remembered a book she'd once read, in which the hero, after his first night with the heroine, had strewn the bed in red rose petals as the heroine slept, and when she woke up he'd made love to her on those crushed petals.

That wasn't this.

They were virtual strangers and it had to stay that way.

As Lulu considered these facts all the bright, unexpected lights he'd lit inside her began to go out, one by one, until she was just anxiety-ridden Lulu again, naked and suddenly cold, with her options few and regimented.

It was time to pull herself together—and, really, she had to get out of this bed and wash and put on clothes.

Feeling a little shell-shocked, despite her best intentions, she slid out of bed, opting to pull the eiderdown around her, and waddled over to join him at the window.

She didn't know the etiquette in these situations. What people did and didn't do. She couldn't even imagine what it would be like to do this so regularly you had a script for it.

He looked down at her with a smile. 'You need to get dressed, *querida*.'

Her chest felt oddly hollow. 'Alejandro, we need to talk.'

'*Si*, we do.' He reached out and curved a hand around her neck, pressed a kiss to her astonished mouth.

Lulu melted into him and the eiderdown slid to her feet. When he released her she was trembling.

'We really need to get a move on, *lucero*,' he smiled.

'Oh, right…yes.' She stepped away from him, trying not to be too embarrassed about her nakedness as she heaved up the eiderdown, but Alejandro fetched her robe and draped it around her instead.

It was such a lovely gesture her heart contracted.

'Alejandro, there's something I need to ask you.'

He looked amused. 'Go ahead.'

'Please don't say anything to anyone at the castle.'

He stilled. 'Say anything?'

'About last night. About us.'

'Why would I say anything?' he asked slowly.

'I don't know. It's just I don't want people to know anything happened. It's private.'

'Yes, it is private.'

She relaxed a little, moistening her suddenly dry lips. 'Then we're on the same page?'

But he was frowning at her. 'What exactly is the problem here?'

Lulu hesitated. She had known deep down it wasn't going to be that easy, but putting it into words made her feel so ineffably sad. 'It's just that we're not going to see each other beyond this weekend.' She looked at anything but him as she said it. 'I don't want people speculating about us and what happened last night.'

She took a peek at him. His expression had relaxed and he touched the underside of her chin to have her meet his eyes. 'What I said last night, Lulu, about it just being one night—I was too hasty. I want to see you again, *hermosa*... can you doubt it?'

Misery rose up to flood her as she realised he was saying the words any other woman would be thrilled by.

But that sense of incredible well-being this man had instilled in her was fast being swamped by panic.

'I can't,' she choked.

'Is there someone else?' His eyes hardened, only to grow more probing as she shook her head.

'You might have changed your mind,' she said softly, averting her eyes, 'but I haven't. I was only looking for last night.'

'Are you sure?' His voice was coaxing, as soft as hers, but about a hundred times deeper and rendered incredibly sexy by his accent.

He didn't believe her, she realised. Probably because any normal woman in her position would fling herself at him. The problem being *she* wasn't normal...

'I can't,' she said, stepping away from him. 'Please don't push, Alejandro.'

He just stood there, watching her, his arms by his side, clearly trying to work her out. Lulu wanted to tell him not to bother. It was really terribly simple—she was too much trouble. He just didn't know that yet.

'You know I will try to change your mind this weekend?' he said, in that beautiful, coaxing voice she needed to block out.

Lulu wanted to stopper his mouth. He had to stop saying these wonderful, thrilling things to her. He had to be made to see she wasn't worth the trouble.

'No, don't do that, Alejandro. Please. I don't want you touching me or acting—acting in any way towards me that might be construed as intimate.'

It had come out all wrong, and she could feel her chest growing tight as a drum as he regarded her in newly tense silence.

'My friends and family are going to be there and they'll only ask questions,' she finished, half under her breath, unable to meet his eyes.

Alejandro discovered he didn't much like being put in the interesting position of being a woman's dirty little secret. Although at least it would explain the stone lodged in his chest.

It was also a reminder to him that the moment you expected something better from a woman was the moment she let you down.

'Please don't be difficult about it,' she said.

It was the bare shoulders, he decided, and the inky curls out of control above them, and her mouth, still swollen from kissing him. That was what was rubbing him up the wrong way.

As soon as they were back in the real world this feeling of possessiveness about her would loosen and fall away. There were plenty of beautiful women out there.

'There is no difficulty, *querida*. I'm just surprised. You didn't seem like that kind of girl.'

'What kind of girl?' she framed uneasily.

'A woman who was looking for a one-night stand.'

A flash of real hurt glanced across her face, but she merely looked away and didn't deny it, and Alejandro discovered that all his reasonableness in this situation was gone. He wanted to destroy something.

He'd slept with a lot of women as a younger man who just wanted to score a little fame and it hadn't bothered him, because he hadn't been in it for anything other than the sex.

But inexplicably the woman who came to mind was Valentina. He could still see his ex-wife—then his very *current* wife—clutching a sheet to her breasts while her lover, his erstwhile teammate, yanked on clothes so at least he would be dressed when Alejandro knocked him out cold.

In the end he hadn't swung that punch. The guy had done him a favour—had destroyed whatever his parents' crazy marriage had left of his faith in an old-fashioned till-death-do-us-part relationship.

When he'd asked Valentina why she'd married him as they'd signed the divorce papers she'd said simply, 'You're a ten-goal player.'

He looked at Lulu now—at her closed expression, her tightly held mouth.

Was that what this was about?

He remembered how she'd been on the plane: spoilt and demanding and exactly the kind of woman he avoided like the plague. He grimly reflected on the efforts he'd made in the past with Valentina, to satisfy her endless demands for a different life while holding together the livelihoods of everyone on the *estancia*. He'd wasted two years on a woman who was empty inside and had blamed him for it. He wasn't wasting any time here.

He grabbed his bag and shoved a few things inside. 'We need to get a move on,' he repeated calmly.

Lulu watched Alejandro zip up his bag, utterly together, as if something very special *hadn't* just been smashed at their feet.

She guessed he did things like this all the time, whereas

she'd only done it once—now, with him—and it felt so strange and emotional and...*knotty*.

The problem was she couldn't explain the circumstances of her request any more than she'd been able to explain why she hadn't been able to give up her seat on the plane.

But she wanted to.

She opened her mouth to ask if he could think of another way, but what was the point? What was she going to ask of him? That he sneak into her room at night when no one would see? It was too ridiculous, and he'd just laugh at her or—worse—see her as odd and damaged. Better he think she could turn off her feelings like a tap, that last night had meant nothing to her. Because she had to let this go.

One day, when she was better, she'd be able to handle a relationship, but not now. She just wasn't ready yet. Certainly not this weekend.

'You might want to get dressed,' he said.

His expression was cool, but she couldn't blame him for it.

'Our transport's here.'

'Transport?'

She followed his gaze out of the window. And she forgot about feeling about an inch high. She forgot about feeling in the wrong. Forgot everything but the need to hold herself upright by clinging onto the windowsill.

There was a stonking great black helicopter sitting on the hill.

Leaving the bed and breakfast, Alejandro peeled off a couple of large notes to cover the picture they'd knocked off the wall and the broken lamp.

Mrs Bailey gave them a knowing look. 'Not married long, then?' she said, and Lulu wanted to die.

If she'd been a normal sort of girl it would have been funny. This morning would have been the start of something wonderful—but it wasn't.

Instead she felt all knotted up inside, and with a murmur of goodbye and thanks she hurried outside, insisting on carrying her own case.

Perhaps it was foolish to ask him what he'd said to Mrs Bailey, given the mood between them.

'Why would she think we were married?' she asked as he led the way across the gravel to dump their luggage in the car.

According to Alejandro, a staff member from the castle would be driving his car in for him. If she'd needed any indication beyond a *helicopter* that Alejandro occupied a different stratosphere from her, his casual expectation that employees would take care of things settled the issue.

He opened up the boot, grabbed her bag and dropped it in.

Lulu bit her lip to stop herself from mentioning the crystal...

'I didn't say anything, *querida*, if that's your question. I think it must have been all the noise you were making.'

With that he flashed her a challenging look, locked up the car and led the way towards their behemoth transport.

It was a short and thankfully uneventful flight before Dunlosie Castle came into view.

The place Lulu had been so anxious to reach yesterday was now the last place she wanted to be. All she wanted to do was lick her wounds in private. But at the same time she was so frustrated with herself she could scream.

She gazed out over the view of the nineteenth-century castle built around the original twelfth-century ruin on the shores of a loch, still smarting from his words.

He might be angry with her, but he didn't have to make her feel self-conscious about making the wrong sounds during sex. She couldn't help the sounds she made. Any more than she could help it that she was not going any further with him.

'As far as wedding gifts go,' he drawled, 'it's a jaw-dropper.'

She whipped her head around, because it was the first thing Alejandro had said to her since they'd boarded.

'What wedding gift?'

'Khaled gave Gigi the deeds to the castle last night.'

Lulu bit her lip and for an awful moment wondered if her best friend was going to up sticks and move here.

'Want one?'

What? Lulu didn't know how to answer that. Of course she didn't. But it was impossible to read him, so she wasn't sure if he was having a go at her again.

Well, he could believe what he liked. About her being jealous…about her wanting the things Gigi had. Even if she did.

She did.

She dragged her eyes off his hard expression.

Only they weren't the things he *thought* mattered to her.

How on earth had they been as intimate as they had been last night and yet they still seemed to know nothing but superficialities about one another?

Because you want it that way, Lulu. It's more comfortable for you.

She pushed that voice away. She couldn't help her condition.

Isn't it convenient, though, that it's there? You don't have to delve a little deeper and look at what's really going on here.

Lulu tensed, and that horribly familiar twisted feeling started up in her belly. By the time they landed the feeling was getting worse by the second.

It wasn't helped when, as they disembarked, Lulu's attention was caught by the woman who was coming towards the helipad across the lawn. The one person she really didn't want to see right now.

In her distress she almost lost her balance, but Alejandro had her and for a moment didn't seem about to let her go.

She looked up in alarm.

He had to let her go!

All she could see was the uninhibited things they'd done together last night.

And he was about to meet her mother!

Félicienne would make a fuss, and then Alejandro would know the truth about her, and she just couldn't bear that.

'Take your hands off me,' she hissed, and after a long look he let her go. She turned away from the expression on his face because it made her feel like a horrible person.

She wasn't horrible—she was just having a very bad day.

Pulling herself together, Lulu took off across the lawn, her attention fixed on her mother, who had that frantic look on her face—as if her only daughter had been off trekking down the Amazon, not taking a short flight from Paris to Edinburgh and staying overnight in a nearby village.

She could imagine Alejandro behind her, looking big and rugged and exactly the kind of man her mother would shrink from. She really, *really* didn't want them to meet, and the faster she moved the better chance she had of keeping her two worlds from colliding in the worst possible way.

Only she was shaking so hard she thought she was going to fall down.

She stumbled.

'Lulu?' Alejandro was at her elbow to steady her, but she pulled away as if he'd touched her inappropriately.

'I told you to leave me alone!' she cried, her distress making her shrill. 'What don't you understand about that? I don't *want* you!'

Alejandro's big body tensed but he let her go. 'Fine,' he said simply.

Which was when she finally lost control of her legs, wobbled and collapsed headlong in a heap in the grass.

CHAPTER TEN

'SHE'S FAKING IT,' Khaled said dismissively, pouring them both a couple of fingers of whisky.

Alejandro had been telling himself exactly the same thing, but hearing it coming from another man pulled an aggressive response out of him.

'You didn't see her,' he said grimly. 'Something's wrong.'

Khaled gave him a long look. 'Good trip, then?'

Alejandro knew he should put it aside. He didn't want to discuss Lulu and it had nothing to do with her plea for discretion. He felt protective of her, and he didn't do protective. It left you open to manipulation, and the last time that had happened he'd almost lost the *estancia*.

No, he was here to enjoy the weekend. To watch his good friend make official the relationship that had intrigued Paris since the cabaret Khaled had won in a card game had hit the headlines and a red-haired showgirl had come into his life.

Alejandro had been at that game. He might have won that hand. He might have met that showgirl. But the one who swam to mind had glossy black curls and big brown eyes and the sweetest raspberry-tipped breasts.

He rubbed at his temples. It wasn't just Lulu's body that was playing havoc with his thoughts.

No, what really bothered him was the way she had felt, flopped in his arms as he carried her inside. She'd behaved so erratically this morning...as if she'd been struggling with something he hadn't been able to see and then it had seemed to overwhelm her.

When her mother had intervened he'd felt aggravatingly powerless, and for a man who made sure he called the shots it had been an unsettling position to be in. But what right did he have to interfere? Why in the hell would he *want* to?

Lulu had made herself very clear on the subject. Besides, he knew well enough what happened when you went riding to a woman's rescue.

The tension in him deepened.

'So why aren't you down there, mopping her brow?'

Khaled appeared to be enjoying this, and Alejandro found himself wanting to hit something. Probably not a good idea if it was the groom, a day before the wedding.

'Her mother appears to have it covered.'

'Probably a good thing. Gigi wouldn't be happy with you making a move on her friend.'

Alejandro straightened up. 'Why's that?'

'Lulu's special.' Khaled sipped his whisky, looking at home in this draughty pile of stone.

'Special?' Alejandro discovered his pulse was beating hard in his ears.

'Sheltered, wrapped in cotton wool by her parents, not much idea of the real world. I doubt she's ever had a boyfriend.'

The glass he held dropped through his fingers and smashed on the stone.

Khaled raised an eyebrow. 'That answers *that* question. Man, you'd better hope Gigi doesn't find out.'

'He scooped you up and carried you inside…it was so romantic,' enthused Trixie. 'It was like something out of *Gone with the Wind*—you know, when Rhett carries Scarlett up those stairs.'

'To force himself on her,' scoffed Susie. 'Yes, really romantic.'

'Rubbish—no one forced himself on Scarlett,' Trixie shot back. 'Remember the smile she had on her face the next morning?'

Lulu wanted to die. She didn't remember Alejandro carrying her inside. She only knew where she was now, as her mother's face swam into view, and then she heard Gigi making everyone clear the room.

Fortunately that meant only Gigi heard her mother begin to cross-examine her about taking her sedatives and why she'd thought she was capable of flying alone in the first place.

The urge to scream at her mother was strong, held back by Gigi's eyes telegraphing rescue over Félicienne's narrow shoulder, and then her suggestion that the older woman might organise some tea while she and Lulu talked.

Gigi had always been able to manage her mother.

'You'll feel better when you've had a cup of tea,' Gigi said gently, for Félicienne's benefit.

The moment the door closed Lulu struggled upright.

'I'm sorry, Gigi. I'll do better.'

'What are you talking about?' Gigi took her hands. 'You're doing fine.'

'I'm supposed to be making this the best weekend of your life, and so far all I've done is cause mayhem!'

'Lu, tomorrow's going to be perfect, whatever happens. It's all good. Calm down.'

'It's your *wedding* day.'

'We said "I do" in a registry office almost six months ago. This is the cherry on top. Nothing is going to ruin this wedding.'

Gigi looked and sounded so confident it was hard not to believe her. Responsibility for running the cabaret and her life with Khaled had given her a new maturity and calm Lulu could only envy.

It just made her feel more of a mess. It threw the events of this morning into relief and brought home to her just how badly she'd handled herself.

'So what's going on with Alejandro?'

'Nothing.' She swallowed.

'He was pretty concerned, Lu, when you hit the grass.'

'Was he?' She hated the way her heart lifted. 'We didn't get on at all,' she lied. 'He made me change a car tyre.'

'He what?'

'The tyre that blew out on our car—I changed it.'

Gigi was grinning at her. 'So you showed him your skills? Nice, Lu.'

Lulu thought of what else she'd shown him and she could feel all the colour in her body meeting in her cheeks.

She was aware of Gigi watching her closely.

'So last night—?'

'We stayed in a bed and breakfast just out of town,' Lulu supplied, studying her sleeve.

'And?'

'It was surprisingly comfortable.'

'Lulu, what happened last night?'

I seduced him.

'Last night's over now,' she said briskly. 'I want to talk about the wedding.'

'Oh. My. God…' Gigi breathed. 'You *slept* with him.'

'No.' She bit her lip. 'Maybe. A little bit.'

'Lulu!'

'Stop making such a big deal of it. I *am* over twenty-one.'

'So what happens after this weekend? Are you together now?' It was impossible to miss Gigi's hopeful interest.

'No, it was just one night.' Lulu couldn't meet her best friend's eyes as she said it.

'One night? Lulu, it was your first time.'

'No, it wasn't,' she mumbled. 'I told you—I lost my virginity to Julien Levolier from dance class when we were both eighteen.'

She raised her eyes to find Gigi looking so doubtful she almost confessed the truth—she'd made it up to get the other girls off her back.

'I didn't believe you,' Gigi admitted. 'I thought you'd made it up.'

'Honestly.' Lulu fiddled with her sleeve. 'I *can* be sexually liberated, Gigi.'

'No, you can't—well, you haven't been until now. Why aren't you seeing him again?'

'It's not that sort of thing.'

Gigi's eyes narrowed. 'Is that what he said?'

'No, it's what we decided together.' Of course that wasn't strictly true either, but the truth stuck in her throat—*I was a coward... I insulted his pride... I messed up.*

Gigi was quiet for a moment. 'You don't want Alejandro to know about your panic attacks,' she said quietly.

Lulu opened her mouth to deny it, but what was the point? Gigi knew her too well. 'It's not his business.' She looked her best friend in the eye, willing her to disagree. 'It's not anyone's business but my own.'

Gigi squeezed her shoulder but was smart enough not to push. A little part of Lulu wished she would push.

Wedding talk eased them away from the difficult subject, but at length Lulu couldn't help circling back in on the thing that mattered most to her and asked, 'Did Alejandro say anything earlier? When I passed out?'

'He was pretty concerned, Lu. But Félicienne told him you had a little medical condition.'

'What?' Could it get any worse?

'You're going to have to tell him something.'

No. No, she wouldn't be telling him anything.

The other bridesmaids filled her in as they dressed for the wedding rehearsal dinner.

'He's like a polo *god*,' explained Susie. 'He's won everything, and people pay a mint to watch him play.'

'I couldn't believe it when I saw him getting out of that helicopter,' added Trixie, fanning herself. 'I knew he was coming, but in the flesh he's just so much *more*.'

'What about that footage of him taking a string of ponies into the surf on that Patagonian beach last year?' said

Susie. 'No shirt. Just muscle and horseflesh. It melted the internet.'

There was a hum of appreciation which left Lulu feeling cross.

'How would you feel if someone took a picture of you at the beach and put it on the internet so that desperate men could salivate all over it?' she grumbled.

Susie laughed. 'It's just publicity, Lu, and he'll be used to it…what with his father and all.'

'His father?'

'Ferdinand du Crozier—international playboy. He broke up a famous Hollywood actress's marriage years ago and then he was seen a week later cruising the Med with her children's nanny! All while he was married to Alejandro's mother.'

'Any publicity is good publicity,' dismissed Adele. 'Anyway, nowadays Alejandro is virtually a brand. You can buy luggage with his polo team's imprimatur on it. How do you think he bought himself a state-of-the-art helicopter?'

Lulu had assumed it was leased. It appeared she'd assumed a lot of things. She was still trying to wade through all this information and work out if it was Alejandro or his father who had seduced the nanny…

'Booooring!' sang out Susie from the bathroom. 'Who cares about what he's worth? He's a sexual athlete. I would have nailed him.'

A sexual *what*? Lulu's chest hollowed.

'Women throw themselves at him. I know he's gorgeous, but it's demeaning, don't you think?' said Trixie. 'Pushing yourself on a man…him knowing it's because he's famous?'

The other girls' gossip, which had battered her a moment before, now sent her stomach cold.

Dieu, was that how he viewed last night? Some desperate woman chasing him because he was famous?

'He dates the most beautiful women in the world—he wouldn't be interested in any of us.' Trixie sighed.

'He does have a reputation for slaying some pretty impressive names,' agreed Adele. 'His last girlfriend was the daughter of a high-profile British politician—she worked for the UN.'

The UN?

Trixie slipped an arm through Lulu's. 'You weren't feeling too crash-hot when you got here, were you, darl? How are you feeling now?'

'Better.' The other two bridesmaids were looking at her expectantly. 'I'm getting over a virus,' she trotted out, feeling wretched.

'Something happened,' she heard Trixie say as she went into the next room to change.

'Nothing happened,' came back Susie's response. 'We're talking about *Lulu*.'

Everything happened, Lulu thought, hanging her head, only it wouldn't happen again.

Dressed an hour later, with her hair drawn up in an Edwardian-style bandeau—the dress code for today was *Downton Abbey*—Lulu walked the vast corridors, went down the stairs and into the dining room, where they would be assembling in half an hour.

With each step she compounded her doubts. She'd barely kept it together after her disastrous arrival. Stumbling out of the helicopter, making it a few paces and then crumpling like cellophane.

If Alejandro hadn't already wiped his hands of her he wouldn't be looking her up after this.

What was worse was that she couldn't talk to Gigi about any of it.

Tomorrow was the Big Day.

It had to be perfect. It had to be all about the bride.

And what had she done on arrival? Set the tone for the whole weekend with her mother running to her rescue.

She understood why her *maman* was so protective. After leaning on her when she was at a young age, now Félicienne only wanted her to have the best of everything and to be safe. But her cossetting wasn't helping her overcome her anxiety. It only added to it.

And this morning she'd been so scared of what her parents might say or do, and of how Alejandro would react. So she'd insulted him and wrecked any chances of them being together at all this weekend, and then she'd leaned on Gigi and used her to handle her mother.

Nothing had changed. And nothing would ever change if she didn't face her fears.

She'd come here this weekend determined to change her life and she'd been doing so well. Last night she had moved past her fear and it had been wonderful. And yet this morning she'd fallen back into the old patterns.

Lulu pulled out the chair she'd be seated in this evening and sank onto it, resting her head in her hands. What was she going to do?

Her phone began to play its jaunty tune and, stirred from her painful thoughts, Lulu reached into her purse.

It was just a text from her mother, telling her she'd come to her room and seen she wasn't there, and she wanted to know where she was and if she was all right.

Lulu was tempted to throw the phone across the room when she sensed movement behind her.

A group of men were passing the dining room and Lulu's ears pricked up. She recognised those rich, low tones. Holding on tight to the phone she'd wanted to hurl, she edged towards the doorway and watched Alejandro, magnificent in formal evening attire that was tailored to his powerful body like a glove, as he and Khaled and several other men she didn't know vanished into the billiards room.

He looked nothing like the laid-back guy who had lowered his aviators to meet her gaze at the airport yesterday, or the generous, tender lover who had made her body known to her in ways she'd never even suspected existed last night.

Instead he looked polished, powerful and predatory. The kind of man she would have shuffled to the back of the chorus line to avoid eye contact with back in Paris, because she could never have handled him.

There was surely something dangerous about physical intimacy. It had done something to her usual reserve, shaken everything she believed in, and Lulu found herself following him down the corridor.

But she could hardly follow him into the billiards room. What would she say?

Besides, he was probably already learning from Khaled what a mess she was—all the things she couldn't do—and now he wouldn't look at her as if she fascinated him. He would look at her and see someone who was too much work.

That was when Lulu became aware that she was standing in a dark corridor just feeling sorry for herself.

If anyone had found her there how stupid she would have looked.

Sad little Lulu, scared of her own shadow and too damn gutless—as Susie would put it—to grab the things she wanted most in life. Willing to let a man think she was a shallow narcissist in order to cover up how truly pathetic her life was in truth.

Whatever had passed between them she owed him an apology—and if she couldn't tell him all of the truth, at least she could tell him *something*, so he wouldn't go away thinking the worst of her.

It was easier said than done.

An hour later she watched him making the rounds of the guests, so tall and broad-shouldered, with his tousled chestnut hair tamed and a slow half-smile making him look as if he knew a secret nobody else did. She couldn't seem to get close enough to him to engineer a casual bumping of elbows, and he had made no move to approach her at all since he entered the room.

She doubted he'd even looked her way. She, on the other hand, couldn't take her eyes off him.

Lulu fought off the memories but suddenly they were all she had moving through her mind, drawing her attention to the gentle ache that lingered from last night's unfamiliar activities.

It was her own fault they weren't together now. She'd asked for this.

A braver woman would just go up to him, draw him aside and discreetly make her apology. But all her bravery from earlier seemed to have fled in the face of all these people and his apparent indifference, and now she just felt as if the room was closing in on her.

Her skin was clammy, her hands were shaking, and to make matters worse her mother kept advancing on her with an agonised expression barely hidden behind her practised social ease.

Lulu had evaded her for some time now, by circulating like a good little bridesmaid among the wedding party members and their partners, clutching a glass of champagne she actually hadn't touched. By the time they went into dinner she was a jangled mass of nerves.

She dared another flickering glance Alejandro's way as Gigi rose to announce, just when they were on their third course, that there would be games this weekend.

Amidst the laughter and commentary she was startled when his attention came her way. It was a casual movement. His gaze just seemed to drift over her, and his eyes, when she looked at them, were dark in the candlelight.

For a fanciful moment she was reminded of a leopard, hanging deceptively lazily in the branches of a tree, every muscle in its superb killer's body seemingly at rest. But those eyes...those eyes held pure predatory intent.

Lulu watched Susie touch his arm, leaning across in all

her sexy glory and saying something that made him smile, displaying the easy charm of a man for whom attractive women did and said anything to claim his attention.

It was somewhat disconcerting to see evidence of what she knew would happen. He would move on.

Not with Susie, nor even this weekend, but with someone. And he would forget about her.

But it had never occurred to her she would have to watch other women come on to him this weekend.

The guests were handing a hat down the table, and she was so enmeshed in her thoughts she didn't pay much attention. She obediently shoved her hand in and took out a small folded piece of paper, ignoring its contents as she glared daggers at Susie across the table.

'There are four teams,' Gigi announced, 'and you'll only find the prize if you solve the clues for your team in consecutive order. There's a time limit so—go!'

Chairs scraped...couples paired off. People were taking their champagne with them. There was laughter, a shriek as a girl was swept up into her companion's arms. Lulu's heart sank. It was going to be *that* sort of game.

She could see her mother, saying something to her stepfather and another older woman, and then Félicienne began scanning the room. In a moment Lulu knew she was going to be dragged off with the middle-aged party, as if she were thirteen and not twenty-three.

She watched Susie grab a bottle and was wondering who would be drinking that with her when a hand closed around her elbow.

'Come on,' said a darkly familiar voice in her ear. 'We can win this.'

Alejandro used his big body to block the crowd and the view of her mother as he pushed her into the stream of guests heading out into the draughty hall.

'But you're purple and I'm pink,' she said, her heart hammering, knowing that wasn't the point.

He snatched the paper easily from her fingers and tore it up, along with his own, tossing it like confetti over his shoulder.

'Problem solved—now we're on the same team.'

Lulu felt hope soar up inside her and explode in a cascading spin of light like a Catherine wheel.

He kept her moving, guiding her up the stairs, the warmth of his body bracketing hers. Lulu had never felt so relieved in her life.

She couldn't help looking up at him, to make sure he was with her and it wasn't just some elaborate sensory hallucination she was having.

He pushed her ahead of him into the book-muffled quiet of what appeared to be the library and closed the doors behind them with finality.

Lulu knew he hadn't brought her here for the reason other couples were vanishing into dark corners of the castle.

This was her opportunity to apologise. Even if she couldn't explain.

'Alejandro—'

He advanced on her and Lulu found herself edging backwards, towards an old nineteenth-century desk. A thrill darted through her.

Maybe he had brought her here for exactly that reason.

'If you still want me to be your dirty little secret I'll do it,' he said, with that same ruthless focus that had so unnerved her earlier.

Embarrassingly, she experienced a liquid pull low in her pelvis and she took another backward step.

'No,' she muttered, 'it's not like that.'

'Then how is it, Lulu?'

'All I want is for you to not want me any more.'

Her bottom hit the edge of the desk. She would probably be struck down for her lies, because she did want him to want her—she wanted it desperately.

He leaned in, hot and male and crowding her. It was

highly exciting. The most exciting thing ever to happen to her apart from last night.

'Then we've got a problem.'

She wanted to tell him that, frankly, this wasn't feeling like a problem just at that moment.

'I still want you.'

Lulu made an involuntary sound, embarrassingly a little like a whimper.

His hips nudged hers and she registered that he was powerfully aroused.

'What's the problem?' he growled. 'Worried your mother's going to find out?'

Yes. Yes, she was.

'Certainly not. I'm a grown woman.'

'Then behave like one.'

And there was the challenge—and also the escape route. Because making love he wouldn't be asking questions, and she'd have this—one more time, just one. So many lonely nights stretched ahead for her. She'd have this and she'd apologise and then everything would go back to normal. Well, *her* normal.

In frustration she reached out and pulled on his shirt. A pearl button popped, and then another. Impatiently she ripped his shirt open with both hands, because sometimes life was complicated enough not to have to deal with buttons.

The sound was almost shocking.

He seemed to like the trashing of his expensive clothes, though, because in answer he lifted her back onto the desk, rucking her skirt up her thighs.

Alejandro ran his palms over them, determined not to rush this. They were as long and smooth as he remembered, and he'd been doing a *lot* of remembering. The scent of her stirred his senses: violets and woman.

She wore more cream satin—this time with shell-pink inserts falling to the tops of her thighs, where her stockings were clipped by tiny blue suspenders. Alejandro hadn't known he had a thing for old-time lingerie, but it definitely did something for him—or the woman wearing it did. He smiled at her as he slid his fingers under the satin to stroke her, because it brought back memories, and the old-fashioned cut made her easily accessible to his hand.

Lulu's chest rose and fell rapidly, a gasp spilling from her lips.

His mouth found hers and he bit down gently on her lower lip, feeling her shudder against him.

He caught her hips in his hands and angled her so that he was cradled against her pelvis. She made a little sound of helpless need and began rocking against him.

He lifted his hands to her beautiful hair but she shook her head.

'No, no—keep your hands below my shoulders,' she muttered. She was unbuckling him with shaking hands.

'Sí.' Although right now she could ask for her own damn castle and he'd promise it to her. 'Why?'

She paused to look up and said, quite seriously, 'I don't want to wreck my hair.'

Her hair? It did seem to be some sort of elaborate confection. Alejandro swallowed the laughter moving through him. It was astonishing how much lighter he felt when he was with her. Freer.

'I'm spending the night with Gigi and the other girls. I don't want them to know.'

Her expression crumpled as she appeared to realise the import of what she'd said.

Again with the secrecy, but he didn't care. All he wanted was to feel her against him again.

They could deal with this secrecy stuff later.

He unclipped her suspenders and slid her pretty vintage panties down over her ankles. He stuffed them in his back pocket and then unbuttoned himself—fast.

He slid his hand up her impossibly silken inner thigh

and found her wet and wanting, and so soft he almost disgraced himself there and then. His damn hand was shaking, and he realised Lulu was trembling too. She wanted him just as badly as he wanted her.

The musky scent of sex mingled with the aroma of old books, the leather furnishings and the subtle apricot fragrance of Lulu's hair which he wasn't supposed to touch. He remembered to grab a condom from his wallet and don it before he positioned himself against her and thrust.

Lulu bit his shoulder, and the next sound to come from her was muffled, but he knew he was finding the spot she loved because she clung to him.

'You feel like hot silk,' he told her with a groan as her long legs wrapped around him for greater purchase. 'Lulu, you're so beautiful…this is all I've been able to think about.'

'Me too.'

He arched her over the desk and pinned her hands above her head as he thrust inside her. With each movement he gazed deeply into her eyes, looking for the wonder he'd seen in her last night, and there it was, flashing like the Northern Lights.

He knew he wasn't going to last, and when he felt her contract around him he buried himself deep and followed her to oblivion.

Lulu clung to him weakly as he sat her up, and he realised every ounce of resentment and anger he had felt towards her today had evaporated completely.

He felt nothing but a deep satisfaction.

She was his.

Her gaze remained unfocussed, and he felt a surge of male pride that he could do this to her.

It had to be pride, because if it was anything else he was in trouble.

'Did I make too much noise this time?' She was serious.

Alejandro remembered what he'd said to her in anger and his conscience did something unfamiliar. It kicked.

'I love the sounds you make,' he said huskily, gently stroking the curve of her cheek.

A little smile trembled at the corners of her mouth. It was the sweetest thing.

He cleared his throat. 'How about we go on seeing one another?'

'You mean for this weekend?'

He'd never known a girl so keen to finish something before it even began. In the past she would have been exactly his type of woman. But he didn't want that this time. He wanted more.

'Let's play it by ear.' He knew her well enough now not to push her. 'I know I'm not ready to give this up just yet…' He swiped her lower lip gently with his thumb. 'That was incredible.'

'I want to,' she began, 'but—'

'Lulu,' he interrupted gently, 'stop making something simple complicated.'

Ouf! Lulu's heart sank. If only it *was* simple.

Seen from his point of view, she knew she was behaving absurdly. But the more time she spent with him the higher the likelihood he would work her out. Find out what a little freak she really was.

Still, it was only forty-eight hours…she'd just have to keep him away from her mother.

'Is that a yes?'

Alejandro watched Lulu's pensive expression grow softer and felt that unfamiliar kick to his chest. What *was* it about this girl that undid all his certainties?

'Oui,' she said, and Alejandro was astonished at the feeling that seized him—it was like scoring a goal under pressure.

Then she turned her head, as if listening for something, and froze. It took him another moment to recognise that there were voices coming down the hall.

Lulu began pulling up her bodice, covering those plump

raspberry-tipped breasts he loved, and she looked so adorably dishevelled he knew he had no intention of letting her
spend the night with a gaggle of girls.

She would spend every night of this weekend with *him*.

Alejandro was about to tell her he'd locked the door
when she pressed her hand to his mouth and with a sweet
look whispered, 'I'm so glad you'll be partnering me at the
wedding. I'll see you tomorrow.'

And with those frustrating words she slipped away.

Partnering her at the wedding?

He briefly shut his eyes. *Idiota!* This had just got complicated.

He was about to go after her—only when he looked
down to deal with the condom time stood still for the second occasion on that day.

Thoughts about negotiating with Lulu over the reality
that he already *had* a date for the wedding—someone who
was arriving tomorrow morning—evaporated.

He had a bigger problem.

It had split. The latex had split.

CHAPTER ELEVEN

AS LULU DRESSED for the big day it hit her that she actually had a date for the wedding.

She hadn't thought she minded being the only bridesmaid without a partner. Clearly deep down she did.

But it was more than that. She'd taken a big step forward, and the fact that she'd come this far with Alejandro was simply astonishing to her.

Lulu did a pirouette in the middle of her room, with its tester bed and its wall hangings—staying here was definitely like living in a National Trust property.

She had a date. She had a date. Alejandro was her date!

Lulu clapped her hands together, aware that she was behaving as if she were seventeen again, and going to a concert with a boy she liked. Which had, of course, been her last real date—if you didn't count the circumspect dinners she'd had with the odd man over the years.

That last real romantic experience had fallen in a heap when she'd had a panic attack in the crowd and thought she was going to suffocate. At the time it had been terrifying. But, looking back, she remembered how light-hearted she'd been before the incident, and full of hope. She had her hope back this morning and she was proud of herself for getting this far.

Which got her thinking about how it would be if she was brave enough to take this further.

If she got up the courage to tell Alejandro the truth about herself.

He wasn't a boy—he was a grown man. Surely he could handle it?

If they went forward he would have to know. She couldn't hide it for ever.

He must want this with her—to have put up with everything and still be so passionate and determined to track her down last night.

She was feeling more certain and her heart was light as she laughed with the other girls on the steps of the chapel and then floated up the aisle, her eyes seeking out Alejandro, resplendent in a morning suit beside the groom.

Gregory Peck, eat your heart out.

All the attention in the chapel had turned to the bride, behind her, but he was still looking at her and Lulu knew she'd made the right decision to tell him.

But this was Gigi's day. She would wait until tomorrow.

There was no chance for conversation anyway. The wedding party was swept up in the taking of photographs, but Lulu was aware of him all the time. His expression was resolute. She beamed at him as they stood together beside the bride and groom.

Then, as they were released from their duties by the photographer, Lulu kissed Gigi and bravely began to make her way over to join Alejandro. She knew her actions wouldn't go unnoticed.

But he was already moving off through the crowd of guests waiting for them on the lawn, and as she watched a bright blonde girl in a beautiful yellow dress broke through and made her way over to him.

She held out her hand and he took it. The young woman was chattering to him and he had his head bent, clearly intent on everything she had to say.

'Who's that woman with Alejandro?' she asked Adele, in a voice that sounded remarkably normal, considering.

'His date,' said Adele, and then turned back to her escort.

And with that Lulu's tremulous, sweet world of possibility shattered into pieces around her.

* * *

For the first time in her life Lulu pictured herself making a scene. She would jump to her feet and upend the table, sending crystal and dishes and all the good wine and champagne flying.

She could actually feel the adrenalin pouring into her limbs in preparation. But she wouldn't do it. She wouldn't make a scene on Gigi's wedding day. She would sit here, with her stepfather to her right and her mother leaning across him to ask if she was all right, and pretend nothing was the matter.

She was an expert in pretending nothing was the matter.

So what if she'd had sex with someone else's boyfriend? It happened. She wasn't to blame. *Was* she to blame?

Lulu could feel herself withdrawing back into her shell. She'd heard the other girls talking about men they'd slept with who'd never called, or who had wives and girlfriends they'd conveniently forgotten about in the heat of the moment. She'd heard their painful stories and, yes, she'd felt a tiny bit superior, thinking that would never happen to her. But the first time she stepped out of her comfort zone—*bang.* Alejandro had taken her down like a big game hunter.

A normal woman would have known. Somehow. There must have been signs. But her social life was absurdly confined. She didn't have the experience to be able to tell. She'd believed everything he'd said to her. What kind of moron did that make her?

All her self-doubt was filling her up again. Making her feel useless. Pathetic.

But she caught herself on that downward slope to self-hatred.

No, not pathetic. Stop beating up on yourself. You've done really well this weekend. You've flown in on your own, you've been an indispensable bridesmaid, and come Monday you'll be back in Paris to start your new course at college and life will open up for you.

Only life was currently staring her in the face in the person of his date—one of those blindingly white-toothed, shiny-haired American girls—a girl who clearly hadn't worked out how two-faced her boyfriend was.

It was a relief when the speeches started. As much as she tried to drown him out, Alejandro acquitted himself spectacularly. He had the one hundred and fifty guests in the palm of his hand. His legendary charm was on display. Gigi was laughing so much she had tears running down her cheeks, and despite everything going on in her own life Lulu felt glad it was all working out so beautifully for her best friend.

Not so much for her, though. Because as Alejandro took his seat, with a significant glance her way she chose to ignore, she remembered what she had forgotten in all the inner turmoil. The wedding waltz.

As Khaled and Gigi took to the floor horror settled like stone in her belly.

Was Alejandro going to dance with that other woman?

Who would *she* dance with?

Lulu bent her head. The only wallflower maid of honour in the history of wedding receptions.

She'd possibly hit a new nadir.

But perhaps it was for the best. Lulu wasn't even sure she was going to be able to stand up.

'Lulu.'

Alejandro was beside her, extending his hand. The same hand he'd slipped between her inner thighs.

She wanted to slap it. She also wanted to grab hold of it like a lifeline.

She gripped him. Dug her nails in a little.

The moment his arm came around her his hand settled at her waist. With his other hand in hers she felt all the fury and hurt and confusion rise up inside her, making it impossible for her to speak.

Alejandro had none of those problems. 'I know you're

angry with me, Lulu, but we need to talk in private. In the library.'

Oh, yes, she could just imagine. He'd probably try to ruck her skirts up again... No—nothing doing!

She suddenly wanted to cry. Very much.

'Anything you have to say to me you can say here.' Thank God her voice only shook slightly. 'We won't be in private together ever again.'

His hand tightened at her waist and Lulu wondered, crazily, if he might pick her up and throw her over his shoulder and haul her out of there. But why would he do that? She wasn't Gigi. She wasn't intrinsically loveable. Her limitations meant she wasn't going to have a normal life.

'The condom broke.'

For a moment Lulu was too busy swimming in her self-pity to pay much attention, and when she did she didn't have a clue why he was saying this to *her*. Why had he said 'condom' in the middle of the wedding waltz?

The. Condom. Broke.

The words shot across her mind as if they'd been lit up in fireworks against a night sky.

Understanding scalded her and she stared up into his beautiful, still face. His jaw was like granite.

Now she knew why his expression had been like the Pyrenees all morning.

'How?' she breathed.

'The usual reasons...latex isn't foolproof. There's only a ninety-eight per cent success rate. We're the two per cent.'

Lulu didn't know when she'd stopped dancing. Only knew that they were standing together in the middle of the dance floor while the other couples glided around them and everything she'd taken to be fixed in her life was falling down around her.

The floor seemed to come rushing up to meet her.

'Where are you in your cycle?' He spoke calmly, but his eyes were like flint looking into hers.

'What? I—I don't know.'

'Think.'

Somewhere off to the side, where the old version of her was still standing, she didn't like his tone. But the stripped-down Lulu, grappling to understand what all this meant, was trying to figure out dates.

'Lulu?' he growled.

'I'm a dancer—my periods are all over the place.'

'Great.'

She really didn't like his tone—nor the way he was telling her this in the middle of the wedding waltz. Although she guessed he *had* given her the option to do it in private.

'One week in,' she came up with.

'That's probably the best news we can hope for. You're less likely to be fertile immediately following your period.'

'How did you become an expert on this?' Her voice had grown slightly shrill.

'An internet search and not much sleep last night,' he growled back.

Good, thought Lulu unhappily, *let him suffer.*

'What will happen now?'

'You'll need to contact me if you're pregnant.'

When she thought about last night—lying awake in the champagne-lulled heap she and Gigi had formed on one of the beds, imagining seeing him again, feeling the happiness that had been bubbling up inside her—the realisation now that the only reason he'd wanted to see her again was to check her fertility was almost too cruel for her to accept.

'What a prince you turned out to be,' she whispered, and whirled around and made her way across the hall.

People were staring. Well, let them stare. Gigi was the only one who mattered, and she was so caught up in Khaled she'd never know at this late stage in the day.

Lulu began to run when she was outside the grand hall. She knew where she was going because she had already set down her routine here. The same corridors, the same

rooms. But she found herself pressing close to the walls—
a sure sign that things were closing in on her.

It had been such a beautiful ceremony, and Gigi was so
happy. Everything had gone off splendidly—only for this
news to drop like a bombshell…

But surely she wouldn't be that unlucky?

Lulu found herself pushing open the tall, heavy doors
in front of her and entering the hushed, carpeted surrounds
of the library.

Explicit memories from last night washed over her.

'Lulu, you can't run away from this.'

She jumped, plastering a hand over her chest, until she
realised she was playing the role of a gothic heroine and
snatched it away. 'You *followed* me!' she accused.

'Of course I bloody followed you.' He strode towards
her, so powerfully masculine she couldn't help shrinking
back. 'This is important, Lulu. You can't just push this
away and pretend it hasn't happened.'

'You think I don't know that?'

Was he making a crack about what had happened at the
bed and breakfast?

She backed up against a table, gripped its edge. It only
reminded her more of what had happened in here last night.
She didn't want to think about last night.

'What sort of a man are you anyway?' She didn't give
him a chance to respond. 'Well, I know now, don't I? You
just go from one woman to the next, like a bee to a flower,
only you don't extract anything—' *except for her heart*
'—you just leave deposits.'

'What are you talking about?'

Her *heart*? Really?

Lulu stared at him, horrified. Her heart wasn't involved.
It was her feelings he'd trashed. The bastard did *not* have
her heart!

'You're just like your father. You're a…a philanderer.'

Like his father? Where had that come from? What had she heard? Read?

Alejandro's first reaction as a young man had been to punch in the face any journalist who had come at him with prurient accusations about *like father, like son*. The intervening years had seasoned his reaction down to a cool, half-amused 'no comment' response.

Hearing the accusation come out of Lulu's sweet mouth made it raw all over again.

'You know nothing about me, Lulu, and even less about my father.'

'I know that—and now you're telling me I could be pregnant by a man I'm not married to. How am I expected to react?'

'Try not screeching out the news to all the inhabitants of the castle.'

'I do *not* screech! she shouted, then looked around as if people might come pouring in to see what the fuss was about. 'What are you going to do about it?' she hissed.

Later, when he analysed the situation, Alejandro would recognise that this was the line he should never have uttered. 'I think I've done my bit.'

Lulu looked ready to haul off and punch him, but for some reason he relaxed. Alejandro discovered that with Lulu the hostility was starting to feel like foreplay.

He made the mistake of smiling at the idea.

'You think this is *funny*?'

She was almost dancing on her toes with fury—a little French tornado of outraged sensibilities.

And he felt…surprisingly calm. For the first time all day he felt good—because now they were talking everything felt a lot less fraught. He was beginning to think that if he'd forced her to talk yesterday they wouldn't be facing this problem now. Sex between them was incendiary, and it just burned the reason out of both of them.

His gaze dropped to her pelvis, where she had settled

her hands, as if trying to repel any imaginary seeding in her womb.

He frowned. It wasn't as if he'd been *trying* to impregnate her. But she was glaring at him as if he'd wilfully and wantonly planted a baby inside her. And now he was seeing other things: Lulu's slender curvy shape distended, a little person growing inside her until she was a soft, round, fecund woman, with *his* baby…somewhere in Paris.

This sudden and to his mind bizarre detour of his imagination had him doing a double-take.

He focused on the more important question. Paris was a big city. He didn't even have her address.

Dios.

How the hell had he missed all this?

Logically, he knew he could get it from Khaled. But right now this was about the two of them. He had no intention of involving other people who would by necessity come between them.

She spun away from him.

'Where the hell are you going?' he growled.

She didn't even look around as she flung over her shoulder, 'Away from *you*.'

'Oh, no, you don't, *querida*.'

He seized her by the wrist and Lulu jerked her head round, and for a moment all he saw was the true panic in her eyes. He was so puzzled by it that when she rounded on him with a raised elbow he wasn't quick enough to deflect the blow and it connected with his jaw. His head jerked back and he let her go.

'Damn!'

Pain radiated from his face and around the back of his neck, and when his vision cleared Lulu was nowhere to be seen… And then he saw her knee. Narrow and pointy and shaking. She was crouched behind the desk.

'Lulu?' he said quietly, stepping carefully around the corner so as not to frighten her.

She was huddled there, looking as shocked as he was.

'Mon Dieu!' She pressed her hands to her mouth. 'I'm sorry—I'm so sorry. I didn't mean it.'

He just offered her his hand and after a hesitation she took it.

'I hit you!' she said jerkily, shaking her head as if she needed to clear it of something. Her whole body was trembling.

'You struck out at me—there's a difference.' He wanted to comfort her but was careful not to embrace her. Something had spooked her, and he didn't like the picture it was painting.

She lifted her hand to his chin and tentatively stroked him where a red mark was already appearing. 'You'll have a bruise.'

'It's all right, Lulu.' He covered her hand and she let him.

'No, it's not. What sort of a maniac hits people?'

But she knew. Out of the past came a memory of her father catching hold of her mother, of the way he would shake her. Never a punch, never a slap, never anything that would leave a mark.

Only fingerprints, standing out on her wrist long after he had let her go.

Her mother had always pretended they didn't matter. Would rub her skin. Would hide it.

'Lulu…' She became aware that he was saying her name. Had possibly said it several times.

She looked up at him blindly.

'Lulu, what happened to you?' he asked, with a quiet intensity she'd only seen in him when they were intimate. It focused her.

'I—' She shook her head. 'I can't talk about it.'

She just couldn't, but her hands had curved over his forearms and she realised she was holding tightly on to him.

Why was she seeking comfort from the very man who'd thrown her life into such disarray?

Because…because he made her feel like a bigger person—stronger, *normal*. He made her feel like the Lulu she might one day be.

This man who'd brought another woman to the wedding.

Lulu stepped back, wiping at her eyes and her nose with the back of her wrist. It wasn't very ladylike, but it was all she had.

'Why don't you go and dance with your girlfriend and leave me alone? I'll let you know if there are…consequences.'

'Madeline is not my girlfriend,' he said decisively. 'She's my plus one.'

'Plus what?' Lulu's voice quavered.

'Madeline's an old friend. We've never been romantically involved. I promise you, Lulu. The invitation was for two, it's a high-profile wedding, and she asked if she could come with me.'

Lulu felt like a balloon that just had the air let out of it. She knew in a minute that she would feel relieved, but right now all she could do was stare at him.

'I was going to tell you last night, but you rushed off. Lulu—' He stepped towards her.

'Non!' She glared at him unhappily. 'Don't come any closer. It's never good when you come closer.'

He stopped. Then he ran a hand through his hair and seemed suddenly younger, less the cold stranger he'd been at the reception—the man who had brought another woman to Gigi's wedding and not told her. He was suddenly Alejandro again, but an Alejandro toting a great deal of baggage she hadn't known about—like the fame, and the women who apparently pursued him in droves.

'Dios,' he said. 'This is a mess.'

Lulu couldn't agree more. At least in that they were on the same page.

'We need to get you onto contraception.'

Or not!

'Excuse me? That has nothing to do with you.'

'The hell it doesn't. You could be pregnant, Lulu. If you have unprotected sex this is what happens.'

'As I never intend to have sex again in my entire life, it's no longer a problem,' said Lulu, her chin trembling, 'I was perfectly happy keeping myself to myself, and then you wrecked everything.'

He was frowning at her. He seemed to be struggling to follow her words and she wondered for a moment if her English had clotted up, as it had a habit of doing when she was overwrought.

'What do you mean, keeping yourself to yourself?'

He suddenly seem to loom over her.

'I don't want to talk about it.' Lulu pursed her lips, folded her arms and faced the other direction.

'Dios,' he said, almost under his breath. 'I knew you were a virgin.'

It was the last straw.

'Did you?' she snapped. 'How clever you are. Give the man a medal.'

'Lulu—'

'I was *not* a virgin,' she stated, staring at an old tapestry on the wall, in which a man in armour appeared to be poking a dragon viciously with a three-pronged weapon. She wished above all things she could be doing that to Alejandro du Crozier right now. 'I lost my virginity when I was eighteen—how many times do I have to explain this to people? I just never followed up with anyone else.'

She heard him sigh.

'Not that it's any business of *yours*,' she added. 'Any more.'

'Then why the hell did you decide to follow up with *me*?' He sounded angry again, but in a different way. He sounded as if he cared.

Lulu discovered she disliked that even more. It was just a trick. She whirled around, wishing he would ignore all her ravings and put his arms around her. But he wasn't going to do that.

'And that's the million-dollar question, isn't it?' she shouted—she never shouted, but this was a weekend of firsts. 'Why don't you call me if you ever work it out?'

He'd handled that well.

Alejandro nursed a whisky as he stood at the window of his guest room. The place was draughty, but that probably went with it being several hundred years old, and yet in shirtsleeves he wasn't feeling much except the adrenalin his brain was pumping through his body.

He couldn't put together a coherent picture of her. At every turn Lulu confounded him. She threw up walls, drew lines in the sand for him to step over, made him jump through hoops. She was his worst nightmare.

The kind of woman he'd avoided all his adult life.

A woman who needed drama.

Only she wasn't quite that either... He was missing a piece in this puzzle, and when he had it everything would fall into place.

He couldn't blot out the image of her huddling behind the desk. Hiding. He thought of the story she'd told him of being attacked and wondered if this was the fallout from that. He wanted to take that fear away, and yet he'd given up taking responsibility for other people's happiness years ago, when he knew he couldn't fit the bill.

More to the point, how the hell was he going to handle a baby?

Not that there *was* a baby. Even if Lulu was pregnant she might very well not want to go through with it, which just opened up all kinds of conflicting feelings inside him. He'd always supported a woman's right to choose, but he discovered he had strong feelings when it came to his own potential child.

Was this how his father had felt about the various chil-

dren he'd fathered on the women who had become a big
part of the decline of the *estancia*? Six kids who'd had to
be fed, clothed and educated—along with himself and his
two sisters—and the alimony for his mother had been its
own drain.

But this wasn't the same at all.

He wasn't his father, following every twitching skirt.

True, he didn't ignore his healthy sex drive and live like
a monk, tied to the *estancia*. Women were part of his life
on the circuit. But they didn't interfere with his passion,
which was for horses and winning and seeing his patri-
mony stand strong, as it had for several generations before
his father had almost scuppered it with his extra-marital
affairs and illegitimate children.

Illegitimate children. He wasn't having that either.

Alejandro steeled his resolve.

He knew deep down that he wasn't cut out to be a pro-
tector of anyone. Every time he'd tried to help his mother
as a child she'd pushed him away. His brief marriage when
he was barely out of his teens had hit a wall as soon as it
had begun. As a grown man he'd erected a barrier to protect himself and push others away.

But he couldn't push a baby away. He couldn't ignore
his own child.

He'd been raised by people who did that, and he knew
how heavy a burden it was to carry the knowledge that your
own parents didn't love you through life.

But at least it clarified what he had to do now. He'd solve
all this by taking Lulu with him to Buenos Aires for the
next few weeks. He'd put her up in a nice hotel, look after
her with the best money could buy, do the test with her at
the scheduled start of her period and if she was pregnant
they'd work it out from there.

But he knew one thing. If Lulu *was* pregnant, he'd marry
her and take the consequences.

CHAPTER TWELVE

MOST OF THE guests had departed last night, after the newly married couple had left for the Seychelles, but the rest of the wedding party was still there and he found Lulu among the other bridesmaids and some late-leaving guests in the room off the main hall, saying their farewells and organising their transport back to where they'd come from.

Madeline was long gone, with one of the groomsmen she'd been entwined with the last time he'd seen her, having a very nice time. She'd waved him off when he'd gone over to apologise for his long absence and mouthed, *I'll find my own way home*, which had freed him to focus entirely on the issue at hand: Lulu.

While everyone else was in jeans, country casual, Lulu was dressed to the nines, wearing another vintage outfit— a raspberry-red fitted dress this time, with long sleeves— and she had a bow around her neck to modestly cover the scooped bodice that made her look as if she should be in a nineteen-forties film.

It was Lulu's little waist and neatly rounded hips, rising at the back to her nicely constructed behind, that made her so damn sexy. On her feet she had clumpy black high heels from the same era, and they made her legs look ridiculously slender and long.

Her hair had been teased into a sleek up-do that had his fingers itching to muss it up. Clips glittered like fireflies in the shiny dark mass.

But when she turned around he could see she was wearing sunglasses. Indoors. In Scotland. Now *there* was a statement.

Alejandro knew he was currently standing in a trench called *bastard*, and that he'd dug it for himself.

He couldn't go any deeper, and was tempted just to haul her over his shoulder and carry her out. It did have a precedent. But drawing attention to their situation was hardly the optimum solution at the moment.

He took her aside.

'I've been doing some research. You can take a reliable test on the first day your period's due—which, according to you, puts us three weeks from today.'

He couldn't see her eyes—those bloody glasses—but the tightening of her rosebud mouth said everything.

'I want you to come to Buenos Aires with me. When the time comes we'll take the test and settle the question. Together.'

Her lips parted.

'*We'll* take the test, will we? I think it will be *me* peeing on a stick.'

Alejandro recognised that Lulu had clearly done some self-defence training overnight and knew this wasn't going to be easy.

'If it makes you feel better, *hermosa*, I'll pee in sympathy.'

She glared at him. He might not be able to see her eyes, but her mobile little mouth was doing the expressions for her.

'I'll make it good for you,' he coaxed. 'Put you up in a nice hotel…you can do some shopping. Buenos Aires is big on fashion—right up your alley.' He indicated her pretty frock.

Lulu stared at him in disbelief. She had cried on and off all night. Hence the sunglasses she wouldn't be removing. But, seeing him again this morning, she had felt her blasted heart jump up and down and she'd really hoped he might say something that would make this a little better. Then she would apologise for going off like a firecracker yesterday, and they could talk like grown-ups about how best to handle this.

Only now she'd been pulled into a corner and dictated to. No mention of *them*—it was all about this non-existent pregnancy. Because, really, how unlucky could he be?

Stuck with some girl he'd got lucky with on his drive in to Dunlosie?

He couldn't make it any clearer.

Instead of going out of his way to visit her in Paris, he wanted her to upend her life and go to Buenos Aires and not inconvenience *him*!

Did he really think she was so shallow that shopping for clothes was all she thought about?

Lulu wondered how on earth he'd got her so wrong.

Because he barely knows you. He's not even interested in getting to know you, whispered a caustic voice. *You're just the next girl in a line of girls and he can't move on from you because of a condom malfunction.*

It really wasn't making her feel special.

It was making her angry.

'Why on earth would I come to Buenos Aires?'

'Because I have to work and we have a problem.'

'You may have to work, but so do I.'

'The cabaret season's ended.' At her surprised look he added, 'Your little blonde friend was full of information last night. You're a lady of leisure for the next month.'

This provoked a choking noise.

He glanced at his watch. 'Let's get out of here.'

'No!' She folded her arms. 'I'm not going anywhere with you. I will take a test, and I'll let you know if there's anything that concerns you.'

He glowered down at her. 'What the hell's *that* supposed to mean?'

'Just what I say. I don't need you standing in the bathroom with me.'

Lulu tipped up her chin. It was certainly easier staring him down from behind the shades, and she wished she'd had them yesterday.

'I won't be bullied,' she added, 'and I won't be made to feel I don't have a choice.'

'In what way am I bullying you?'

'Going behind my back, finding out about my schedule. We don't have a relationship, Alejandro, we just have a problem. And I can deal with it.'

He gave her a long, unsettling look. All the more unsettling because, unlike her, he could hide what he was thinking. Then he seemed to make up his mind about something. His mouth curled into a tight smile that somehow held no humour and his eyes searched her face.

'You're right, Lulu, we *don't* have a relationship.'

To Lulu's astonishment her stomach dropped.

'Give me a call if we've got a problem.'

He strode away and Lulu watched him go, unable to credit the disappointment that was dropping through her at a rate of knots.

What was wrong with her? This was what she wanted, wasn't it? He was a control freak. She couldn't believe he'd been scoping out her schedule when she'd thought he was flirting with Susie!

How could he have put her through that?

Lulu blinked. Wait a moment—two nights ago there had been no reason for him to be interested in her schedule. She bit her lip. Unless he was interested in her.

'Chérie?'

Her mother had approached and was looking at her with that half-agonised expression Lulu discovered she could barely look at nowadays.

'I'm flying home today,' she heard herself say, sidling over to the window, which gave her an excellent view of anyone coming and going from this wing of the castle. 'You should stay on with Jean-Luc for the golf.'

'I rather thought you and I could fly down to London for a West End show and some shopping and then shoot home at the end of the week with Jean-Luc—that way I'll be with you if something goes awry.'

Lulu was watching Alejandro cross the courtyard. His long, easy strides were in direct contrast to her own jerking heartbeat. How could he just walk off like that? Although she guessed he *had* tried, hadn't he?

She closed her eyes momentarily, trying to block out her mother's voice telling her how well she'd done this weekend, asking why she'd make it any more difficult for herself by facing another plane journey alone.

Lulu had a sudden image of herself hiding in a hotel bathroom in London, with her mother in the next room, and her peeing on a stick.

She turned around, pecked her mother on the cheek. 'I love you, Maman, but I have made other arrangements.'

'Lulu!'

She grabbed her hand luggage and ran as fast as she could in her clumpy shoes and narrow skirt—out of the room, down the stairs, across the flagstone-laid hall, out into the courtyard.

She was on the lawn when she saw him heading for the helipad.

'Alejandro! Wait for me!'

He turned around, arms hanging loose from those broad shoulders, and Lulu had to swallow a very large lump of nerves. Because he was such a force of nature, so assured in his masculinity and determined to have his way.

Well, so was she. Determined to have her own way, that was. And she was about to take a huge leap into the unknown.

'Why did you ask Susie about my schedule the other night?' she shouted over the *whup-whup* of the blades.

'Because I wanted to date you.'

Finally he'd said the right words.

'I'm coming, then,' she announced. The wind from the

rotors was already destroying her carefully constructed up-do. 'What do you think?'

'You don't want to *know* what I think, *querida*.' His expression was wry. He gave a jerk of his head. 'Get in.'

Lulu scrambled into the chopper. Fresh nerves assaulted her, but she didn't have much choice.

They were already in the air when she thought to look down, and there on the lawn was not only her mother but Trixie and Susie too, all of them gazing skywards. Trixie was waving madly. Lulu extended her hand and waved back, feeling nothing but relief that she was leaving them and their questions behind, but as she turned to Alejandro beside her she felt a big ball of dread in her belly.

So much could go wrong.

Alejandro was looking at her as if he had her exactly where he wanted her. She guessed he did. Only she wondered where the man who had taken her so passionately on the library desk had gone, and she figured that if the idea of an unplanned pregnancy had spooked him, he needed to wait until he'd learned the truth about her.

Too much trouble. Lulu already knew that, and it was only a matter of time until he knew it too.

He'd known if he stopped pushing she would push herself—and she had, Alejandro thought with some satisfaction as they drew up in front of the Four Seasons Hotel in Buenos Aires.

They were right on schedule. He would stash her here and then he could still make his meetings across town, before taking the long drive out to the *estancia* this afternoon.

Naturally he'd keep an eye on her—maybe they could have dinner. Probably a good idea. Discuss their options. What mattered was that she was in town, within easy reach. If she was carrying his baby he wanted to know about it.

Which didn't explain his unease as he escorted her across the square. He was growing distinctly tense as they approached the hotel. Lulu kept looking at him with those big anxious eyes. He should probably explain the set-up.

'You'll be comfortable here—you'll want for nothing, *querida*. You only need to pick up the phone.'

She didn't say a word, but as they walked through the doors and into the lobby of the hotel Lulu slipped her hand into his.

It was a small gesture. No one looking on would even notice it.

Alejandro felt it like a lightning strike.

Her small fingers curled trustingly around his. His mind was back on that Edinburgh street, when she had wound her arms so tightly around his neck and her heart had beat like a trapped bird.

He halted and looked around.

'Alejandro?'

With a nod he turned and strode back the way they'd come, dragging Lulu on her clumpy heels after him.

Alejandro knew he was behaving like a madman. But her small smooth hand in his felt as if she was squeezing something vital inside him.

'What are we doing?' she asked as they stepped out into the warm afternoon and the familiar sounds of his city wrapped around them.

'Sightseeing,' he said.

'Really?'

Instead of being full of disbelief she was beaming up at him as if he'd promised her rubies, not blisters. He paid some attention to her shoes.

'Are they okay for a long walk?'

She looked a little offended. 'You forget, I'm a showgirl—I dance in heels.'

He *had* forgotten. Alejandro just couldn't imagine her up on stage in a rhinestone bikini and feathers. Unclothed, she looked as if she belonged in an eighteenth-century portrait by Goya, *La maja desnuda*.

'Where are we going?'

Her voice broke into his thoughts and he must have looked blank for a moment, because her forehead formed a tiny concertina of indecision.

'Not that we have to go anywhere,' she added. 'Unless this is like a date or something?'

A date? It was the one thing they hadn't had. He'd skipped it all in favour of deflowering her and possibly getting her pregnant. It was wince-inducing stuff.

He could picture the tabloid headlines: *Like father, like son.*

He was *not* his father's son. He had long been his own man. And the press were not going to run with this story.

His hand tightened around Lulu's.

'*Sí*, like a date, Lulu.'

A slow smile curved her mouth. 'It's your city, Mr du Crozier. Where will we go?'

He showed her the historic centre of his town, its cobbled streets with their *belle époque* architecture. He led her into El Ateneo—once a theatre, now one of the most beautiful bookshops in the world.

'I thought this might particularly interest you,' he explained, standing behind her with his hands folded behind his back. 'It was once a theatre where they danced the tango, but tastes changed in the early twentieth century. A local businessman siphoned in the funds to turn it into what you see now.'

She looked up into the domed ceiling. 'What an amazing thing to do—it's like a jewel box for books.' She looked up at him. 'I don't know what would have happened to the club if Khaled hadn't come along. I still shudder to think of the theatre coming down under a wrecking ball if anyone else had been in charge. But, between you and me, I think I would rather like L'Oiseau Bleu to become a bookshop. Only don't tell Gigi.'

'You'd be out of a job.'

'I wouldn't mind so much.' She drifted towards an aisle of books, taking down some volumes on theatre costume.

She wouldn't?

'This is what you're interested in?' he asked over her shoulder, inhaling the gorgeous violet scent of her.

Lulu nodded. 'I've always spent my free time at the theatre hanging around the costumiers. I find it fascinating.' She closed the book and he took it out of her hands to reshelve it. She turned up her face. 'Actually, I'm starting a part-time degree in costume design.' She hesitated, then confided, 'You're the first person I've told.'

Alejandro could see how much it meant to her by the way she searched his face, as if wanting approval.

'That's amazing, Lulu.'

She smiled almost shyly back at him and he had to fight the urge not to kiss her. Then her smile faded and he wondered what she was thinking.

Lulu was trying to picture herself hugely pregnant in front of a sewing machine. She guessed it could be done—other women did it all the time. But she wouldn't be able to work. She would have to rely on…Alejandro. After all her efforts to prise herself lose from her parents she would be back where she started.

'How are you going to fit it in with your showgirl gig?'

Lulu suspected he was implying that working nights and studying during the day wouldn't really be her problem any more *if she was pregnant*.

He clearly wanted to go down that road, so she made herself smile at him and pretend nothing was the matter.

Alejandro saw the light and shadow flickering over Lulu's face. Right now he was struggling to imagine her in a revue. He'd seen the Folies Bergère, and what he remembered was sparkles and bare behinds and jiggling bare breasts.

At the time he'd appreciated it.

Thinking about Lulu that way—in front of an audience of men—just made him hot under the collar.

It also didn't fit with the private, modest girl he knew. The girl who had covered her breasts the first time he took off her bra. He blew out a breath. He really didn't need to be thinking about *that* now.

Instead he looked down at her neat little outfit, at the thirties-style wide-legged green trousers and the cute little cream blouse. She'd changed on the plane en route from Heathrow to Buenos Aires. He found it sexy, but she did also look as if she might be on her way to do the school pick-up—if she was Norma Shearer.

Putting Norma aside, thinking about Lulu as a young mother wasn't a stretch.

Not that any of that was going to happen.

'Well, I dance six nights a week, so there's time during the day when I can go to college. Just about.'

'You dance *six* nights a week?'

'Being a dancer isn't for the faint-hearted,' Lulu replied, clearly relishing proof of her hard work.

He remembered the quick assessment he'd made of her as being spoilt and helpless. He'd been so wide of the mark it made him wonder afresh at his misreading of her. He also acknowledged for the first time what a huge impact pregnancy would have on Lulu's plans.

He raked a hand through his hair. 'I'm sorry, *querida*.'

'Sorry? For what?'

'This situation we find ourselves in. I should have taken better care of you.'

To his surprise she looked slightly irritated. 'I was there too, Alejandro, if you remember, and nobody needs to take care of me. I can take care of myself.'

She turned away and trotted on those clumpy heels towards the doors of the bookshop and out into the busy street, not looking back to see if he followed.

He caught up with her.

'Can't we agree on equal responsibility for the "situation"?' she asked less heatedly as he steered her into a nearby café, where the music was hot and the food was good.

He ordered a lemonade for Lulu and a coffee for himself. 'Agreed.'

He didn't agree. They hadn't been on an equal playing field. Lulu was a rookie—he should have looked after her better.

But he watched her defensiveness fall away at his agreement and acknowledged that her independence was a point of conflict for her. He wasn't sure why. Although after seeing her mother in action with her he could make a stab in the dark at it.

He didn't know much about mother/daughter relationships. His own mother had been about as interested in the girls as a cat. He had only counted because he'd been the heir his grandfather had depended upon and the future source of his mother's income.

He watched Lulu's face as she talked earnestly about her course. It trickled through his mind that his mother might once have been like this, at the start of her modelling career, with the world before her—only to find herself a handful of years later trapped in a marriage she saw as inescapable and taking her misery out on her kids.

But Lulu talked on and on with such determination. He suspected that in the same situation as his mother she would make her own way out, bringing her children along with her.

It made him want to drag her back to the hotel and make her his again. But they weren't doing that. They were having a drink and she was sharing her hopes and dreams, and the fact that they were so simple and yet clearly so profoundly important to her stirred a protectiveness in him he hadn't felt about anyone except his sisters in many years.

He didn't see why she couldn't achieve all she wanted

to. There was no reason why she shouldn't. Except there was that slight wistfulness that crept into her voice as she talked about the various career options her course would open up. As if she might not make it.

'So what will we be doing tonight?'

She brought him back to the here and now with that question. He cleared his throat. 'I'll be working, Lulu, out on the ranch, but I'll drop by when I can.'

Her eyes flew to his and then dropped away.

'I'll organise people to take you out,' he found himself explaining. 'You won't be bored.'

Her face had frozen into a little mask of pleasant indifference. 'I'm sure I won't,' she said tightly, not looking at him.

She put down her glass and started stirring the lemonade with her candy-cane-striped straw.

Alejandro told himself it was for the best. He should be at a meeting right now. She should be back at the hotel.

It was time to wind this up.

'You don't have any luggage,' he said instead.

'No, not even a toothbrush.'

She looked tense, deliberately avoiding his gaze by pretending to watch the crowds go by on the footpath beyond the plate-glass windows. All of a sudden she noisily scraped back her chair.

'I have to go to the ladies'.'

As Lulu dried her hands at the sink she wondered what on earth she thought she was doing.

Alejandro hadn't mentioned this morning that he wasn't going to be around for the next three weeks.

Which was fine, really.

At least he wouldn't witness any of her weird behaviour. She could just sit in her hotel room…

But she wished he'd quit with the confusing messages he was sending.

He kept taking hold of her hand and making her feel like part of a couple, and he'd lulled her into a false sense of togetherness by letting her talk on and on about her plans. She'd definitely relished the opportunity, given that every time she'd seen Gigi lately the talk had always been about the wedding. But mainly it had just been nice sitting together, talking.

She shook her head. Really, he was being very careless with her feelings. Listening to her ramblings, behaving in a protective fashion, making her feel as if she was the only girl in the world. Didn't he know all the nice gestures were making it harder for her?

No wonder she hadn't looked for a sexual relationship before.

Sex made everything so much more complicated.

And it felt awful when it went wrong.

Because it *had* gone wrong. Somehow she'd misread things.

As she came out into the restaurant Alejandro's body language caused what was left of her optimism to drop to her shoes. He looked faintly bored, sprawled in the booth with his phone open while two of the waitresses were clearing their table when it only took one. She couldn't blame them. His long, lean muscular frame was on display in a T-shirt and jeans, but even dressed down he looked incredible, with his tousled chestnut hair falling over his temples.

She hadn't missed the flurry of excitement as their waitresses had recognised him, nor the way Alejandro had dealt with that recognition, erecting a little wall of cool disregard that held them all at bay.

I'm not his girlfriend, she imagined herself telling the drooling girls flitting around him, *but I might be carrying his child. We're doing a test in a few weeks. Peeing on a stick.*

Lulu's pride lifted her spine.

No, she wouldn't be spending time with him.

This wasn't about that.

Besides, it was his loss.

Alejandro shot a couple of emails across town and looked up to see Lulu making her way back towards him.

She could at least smile at him.

He'd changed his plans for her. He'd skipped a meeting this afternoon at his office a few blocks from here, hence the explanatory emails, but he was supposed to be at the *estancia* right now.

She sat down. 'I guess we can go now.'

Alejandro discovered he didn't want to go anywhere.

She wouldn't be alone, he reminded himself. It was the centre of Buenos Aires—the privileged centre. He'd organised a suite for her, he'd hand over a credit card, and with a gym and a pool and a health spa and the Recoleta district just outside, with its high-end boutiques, she wouldn't be bored.

But he knew she wouldn't use the card, and he suddenly felt a deep twist in his gut at the idea of her sitting alone in a hotel room.

She could be at this moment pregnant with his baby and he was planning to dump her in a hotel suite—like a secret he wanted to keep.

He'd be no better than his father.

That decided him—or rather her small hand creeping across the table to touch his did. He slid his fingers between hers.

'Alejandro,' she said, swallowing hard, but her eyes issued a challenge nonetheless, 'I don't want to stay in a hotel.'

'It's all right. I don't want you to either. I'm taking you home with me,' he said.

CHAPTER THIRTEEN

LULU GLANCED AT her phone again and made a face. They
had been driving for several minutes down a tree-lined
road through the property Alejandro's ancestors had held
for centuries—called, evocatively enough, Luna Plateada,
Silver Moon, after the stallion his Scots-born ancestor had
brought across the seas two hundred years ago.

'It's just my mother,' she said, when he asked her what
was wrong.

She hadn't even realised she was frowning.

'Maybe you should put that away,' he suggested. 'We're
here.'

Lulu looked up and she knew in that moment she'd bit-
ten off more than she could chew as she saw the villa loom-
ing up ahead. It was a colonial-style mansion that spoke of
money and history.

It was also a working farm. She'd seen the horses graz-
ing in the home paddocks, and now they drove past brick
stables and various outbuildings into the courtyard.

Lulu took a steadying breath and kept her eyes down as
Alejandro escorted her inside.

There was a lake behind the house. She saw this because
there were glass windows everywhere and an expansive
feel to the house, as if it were open to the outdoors. Moor-
ish arches linked the entrance hall to various other rooms.

Lulu felt a vertiginous sense of dislocation, but coun-
tered it by pressing her back up against the wall as she
stopped in one of the archways.

Staff came trooping past with her luggage.

'How many people live here?' she asked.

'There's eight permanent staff for the house, but they

come in daily, the gauchos who work on the *estancia*, and I keep an office manager here on the estate—he lives in one of the guest houses.'

Alejandro was frowning at her, possibly because she had stuck herself to the wall.

Edging forward just enough not to look completely foolish, Lulu told herself she would cope.

'I'll take you on a tour...'

'No! I mean... I'm tired. Can I go to my room?'

She hated how abrupt she sounded, but it was difficult to speak normally when her vocal cords felt as if they were freezing.

He frowned.

Her phone buzzed.

'Again?'

She shook her head. 'My mother worries.' She read the message.

Alejandro watched her face fall as she read the text and it had his own tension levels knotting. He knew what it was like to be on the end of a tugging string of phone calls and texts. His disaster of a mother couldn't make a decision without dragging him into it. It was probably why he only ever had relationships with women who could take care of themselves.

Lulu clearly couldn't draw that line with her mother. He told himself not to get involved.

Her pleated brow didn't change as she put the phone away.

'Do you want me to throw your phone into the lake?'

Lulu looked up in surprise and then remembered the other night, when she'd wanted to throw her phone across the room. Her mouth trembled into a reluctant smile. 'That might be a bit extreme,' she said.

How had he known?

'Your mother is a nightmare.'

Her forced smile faded. 'How can you say that? You don't even know her.'

'How many times has she rung you today?'

'We're close—I'm her only daughter.'

'I saw her in action back at the castle. She treats you like a little girl.'

'She has her reasons.'

'Your medical condition?'

Lulu's heart began to speed up.

'I'd like to go to my room right now, if that's all the same to you.' She sounded curt even to her own ears. 'It's been a long day.'

'Lulu—'

'No,' she said, her voice rising. 'This is not your business.'

To her confusion he looked as if she had slapped him, when all she'd been trying to do... What *had* she been doing? Didn't she want to change things? But it was so hard, Lulu thought as she followed him closely up the stairs, when your mind and body betrayed you at every turn.

'This is your room,' he said at the top of the stairs, opening the door for her.

'The thing is,' Lulu blurted out, 'when I was looking to push my life in a different direction I didn't factor in pregnancy.'

He leaned back against the door frame. 'It wasn't exactly on *my* radar.'

No, she guessed not.

If the latex hadn't split would she even be with him right now? It was a confrontational thought. Just because he'd come looking for her the night before last it didn't mean anything. He hadn't used any words to her that had even hinted at them pursuing anything beyond the weekend.

He raked a hand through his tousled chestnut hair, stepping closer to her as if he wanted to take things in another direction, and the masculine scent of him tugged on all those new sexual responses she had to him.

'Do you want to talk about it?'

Lulu bit her inner lip. The urge to confide was very strong. To tell him what was going on with her…to share a little of the struggle she faced on a daily basis. But, given he wasn't interested in trying a relationship with her, it was probably not a good idea.

She knew now that she'd misread everything on the eve of Gigi's wedding.

Sex was part of Alejandro's normal life—it wasn't some big deal. She didn't *have* a normal life—let alone a sex-life—and somehow in her inexperience she had made it into something it wasn't.

They were both doing the right thing: waiting for confirmation together. It was good of him to put her up in his home, but it didn't mean she should be holding him hostage to her issues.

It was the house that had thrown her. Managing the space. She couldn't share any of that with him. She couldn't share it with anyone.

Lulu had never felt more alone.

'There's nothing to talk about, is there? We don't know yet—it might all be worry for nothing.' She needed to get out of his sight before she burst into tears. 'I'm really tired, Alejandro…' She turned away. 'Let me go to bed.'

Alejandro found himself standing alone in the hall, staring at Lulu's closed bedroom door.

There wasn't anything more to say, was there?

He'd learned long ago that trying to help someone who didn't want to be helped was a dead-end road. He'd tried to help his mother, and then his sisters to launch their lives free of the *estancia*, but it had earned him nothing from the girls but requests to butt out.

He didn't open himself up like that any more. He'd offered support—Lulu didn't want it. There wasn't much more he could do.

He'd seen her face as they drove up. The way her features had frozen to mask her disappointment. He knew now he should have left her at the hotel.

She'd made it obvious she was uncomfortable here. He had vivid memories of long before his ex-wife had made it clear she hated it there—of his mother, dropping them at the house and then tearing back up the drive in a cloud of dust. But worse had been the times his grandfather had insisted she remain, when she'd closeted herself away in her rooms, from which she'd refused to emerge.

Sí, eyeing Lulu's closed door brought back many memories. None of them good.

He turned away abruptly. He didn't need reminding.

Lulu got up the next morning and ventured across the echoing parquet floors from sumptuous room to room, trying not to hear the silence or look out at the immense flatness around them, rising to low blue hills in the distance.

She felt almost unmoored in large open spaces. They were worse than being locked up in the cabin of a plane. But as long as she could establish a routine here for the next few days and have her touchstones—her room, Alejandro, knowing the people around her—she would do fine.

Only then she discovered Alejandro was gone. She stood in the kitchen with Maria Sanchez, who acted as his housekeeper, and learned that he wasn't expected back until Thursday.

Two whole days!

'He works hard,' said Maria in English, when Lulu asked if he'd said where he was going. 'I tell him his grandfather had his two brothers to help—and he didn't have the pressures of a polo team. But he does not listen. He is like his grandfather that way. He sets his mind on something and nothing will deter him.'

'You've worked for the du Croziers a long time?'

'Over thirty years.' Maria looked proud. 'I came here when Alejandro's grandfather was El Patron. It is a shame he never knew what a success his grandson has made of the *estancia*—especially after that son of his.'

'Alejandro's father?'

Maria made a face. 'Fernandez never cared for the land...never cared for the people here. His grandfather took Alejandro under his wing and sent his parents away. Good riddance, I say. Now we have the best pure-bred Criollos in the country.'

Lulu frowned. 'He sent his parents *away*?'

Maria drew herself up, clearly relishing an audience for her views. 'El Patron could see how it was tearing Alejandro and his sisters Isabella and Luciana apart, watching them fight. Fernandez was never here, but Marguerite aired their dirty laundry to anyone who would listen. People felt sorry for her, because of Fernandez and his women, but she manipulated everyone with her weakness. A real woman works. Instead she liked the easy money.'

Lulu thought of her own mother, married at eighteen with no job skills. Married to a man who had only shown his true colours when she'd had a small child and another one on the way and had been trapped.

Félicienne had remarried now, and she worked. She had her own flourishing import business. She'd never be trapped again.

'Are you his sweetheart?'

'P-pardon?' Lulu stammered.

'Alejandro doesn't bring his women here. Yet *you* are here.'

'I'm not his sweetheart...um...girlfriend.' Lulu knew she was babbling, but what did Maria mean by *his women*? 'I'm not anything.' Which was a sobering thought.

Lulu discovered that she felt even more unmoored.

'You are something,' said Maria wryly, and turned towards the oven.

Lulu moved faster, slid on oven mitts and opened the oven.

'Gracias.'

Lulu stayed in the kitchen, helping Maria prepare the food. It was easier than explaining why she didn't want to go outside.

She told herself she would venture out tomorrow. She just needed to get her bearings.

She also needed a routine for her meals—something Maria was agreeable to after all her help in her kitchen.

The three weeks stretched out interminably. There was no way she could hide her problem for that long. There would be an incident, and Alejandro would witness it, or somebody else here in the house, and they would tell him, and she would be humiliated, and—baby or no baby—he wouldn't want her.

Nobody would want to be around her. Whatever happened, he wouldn't want her when he found out.

There was a problem with his champion stallion, Chariot. According to the phone call Alejandro had got that afternoon the old boy was still limping, and he wanted to have a look at that injured fetlock himself. It was the only reason he'd walked out of a reception for the team in one of Buenos Aires's better hotels tonight and torn up the highway to home.

At least he told himself that.

By the time he was striding through the house he'd heard from Miguel Sanchez, his steward, that Señorita Lachaille had not wanted to be shown around the *estancia*. That in fact no one had seen her emerge from the house for two days. From Maria he learned that Lulu wasn't sick, but that she appeared to prefer to eat her meals in her room.

His housekeeper didn't seem to think this was a problem—which was unusual, as Maria complained about most things.

He took the stairs by threes, then stood at Lulu's door.

His door.

The guest room door.

Memories swamped him. Of sitting slumped at another door, listening to his mother crying on the other side. Of his mother sending for him to relay her complaints about the food, about the way she was being treated.

His hand hovered over the door. He wanted to thump on it, but if Lulu was exhibiting behaviour that pushed his buttons he knew he didn't have all the facts.

He knocked softly. 'Lulu?'

Nothing.

He knocked more heavily. Again nothing. He pushed it open and stepped inside.

Ten minutes later it was apparent that she wasn't in the house.

'Check the outbuildings,' he told the men he'd gathered in the courtyard.

He eyed the lake and told himself he was being overly dramatic.

He was crossing towards it when he saw the light in the high gable of the brick stables. Nobody was supposed to be in there. Chariot was in there. He'd given orders.

Lulu?

His chest was tight with adrenalin as he slipped through the half-open door, his tread light on the gravel. If it wasn't Lulu, then someone was in there illegally. There was several million euros' worth of horseflesh alone in these stalls.

It was dark and quiet, but around the corner a light shone over Chariot's stall.

He heard the light murmur of her voice. He'd have known it anywhere, even if she hadn't had that French accent, sexy and flowery with all those soft *V*s.

As Alejandro drew closer he realised she was talking to someone. He stopped.

'You have to stay there. If you come any closer I don't know what I'll do.'

Every muscle in his body tensed. Was someone threatening her?

'*Bien*, be a good horsey and let me pass. If you don't I know what happens from experience—and it's not good. You really don't want be around me when I lose it. And I *mean* lose it. No one wants to be around that.'

He stepped around the corner and looked over the stable door. Chariot was standing quietly, rocking a little from side to side, and Lulu was pressed up against the far wall, eyes huge, face white. There were traces of blood on her blouse and scratches on the fine skin just below her collarbone, which worried him, and she was cradling something to her breast.

'Lulu?'

She looked up and relief swept over her face, but she kept herself plastered against the stable wall.

'It's all right, *hermosa*,' he said in a quiet voice. 'Just stay where you are. I'm coming in to get you.'

'That would be good…' she choked.

Chariot lifted his head at Alejandro's familiar scent. 'Hello, boy…nice and easy. I'm just taking the lady with me. You've got that lovely harem and this one is mine.'

The moment he was between her and Chariot, Lulu sidled behind him and he backed her out of the stall, keeping his eye on the stallion.

Anyone else and he would have had no sympathy.

There were *signs*. Any damn fool would know enough not to enter a stallion's stall. Chariot's mood was dicey, at best, and with an injured fetlock he wasn't making friends at the moment. One of those hooves, precisely placed, could have knocked the life out of her.

But when he turned around Lulu was crouched on the ground, head bent.

He was beside her in an instant.

'Can't breathe...' she gasped.

He settled her back, only to realise she was still cradling something against her breast. He disengaged what turned out to be a newborn kitten from her hands and, at a loss as to what to do with it, slipped it into his shirt pocket. Then he returned his attention to Lulu, who had drawn her knees up. He gently encouraged her to keep her head between them while he rubbed her back in concentric circles, counting breaths for her. All the while she made wheezing sounds that sent him cold.

When her breathing was less laboured she lifted her face. 'Oh...' she said, and reached out gently to touch the head of the tiny creature hanging over the side of his pocket, its blue eyes barely open.

He was beginning to get a picture of why Lulu had been in the stall. 'I believe you two are friends?'

Lulu insisted on wobbling to her feet, with his help, and indicated the neighbouring empty stall. 'They're in here,' she said.

Sure enough there was a barn cat, with a litter of four kittens lying in a nest of fresh, fragrant hay. Lulu restored the fifth to the pile. They couldn't be more than a few hours old.

She stood looking down at them. He noticed she had colour in her face again, but the expression in the eyes she lifted to his took him off-guard. She looked almost jubilant.

'I *did* it,' she said.

'Did what?' he asked huskily. 'Rescued the kittens?'

'Managed...' She bit her lip. 'Almost.'

He gave in to his frustration with her. 'You could have been *killed*.' His voice was hoarse, as if he'd been yelling. But he never raised his voice. He'd grown up with adults for whom screaming matches had been part of a daily ritual.

Lulu made a face. 'I know. It was stupid. But I was passing and I saw the light on. I wanted—I wanted to pat the horses.'

'You wanted to *what*?'

She sank down into the hay, as if her legs weren't going to hold her, and he remembered she'd had a significant fright. Hell, he wasn't feeling so crash-hot himself. Seeing her pinned up against that wall...

'I saw the cat at the rear of his stall with her kittens and I had to get them out.'

'You mean you went in more than once?'

'Three times.'

His gaze dropped to what he could see of her chest, crisscrossed with scratches. He hunkered down and took hold of her hands, equally bloodied, pushing up the long sleeves to find her wrists red and white with raised welts.

'*Dios...*'

'I'll mend,' she said, almost impatiently, pulling her hands back.

'Woman...' he breathed, and the urge to shake her was subsumed in the need to hold her close. He dragged her in tight against him. She came.

'What made you come out here so late in the day?' he asked, holding her so that she rested against him in the hay.

'I wasn't ready until now,' she said haltingly.

'Ready for what?'

He looked at her as if she was speaking another language. Another minute of this and he was going to look at her as if she was a complete flake.

Lulu swallowed hard. She could convince herself that she had to tell him the truth now because whatever happened he was going to think she was crazy anyway. Or tell herself that he'd just rescued her and she owed him an explanation.

But right now what she really wanted was to tell him

the worst thing about herself and hope he might overlook it and see the woman beneath.

'I have an anxiety condition.'

Put like that, it sounded utterly underwhelming. But Alejandro was looking into her eyes as if what she was telling him was of the utmost importance. It gave her the courage to continue.

'It's a form of agoraphobia.'

'A fear of open spaces?'

'No—that's a common misconception. I have panic attacks if I'm in a situation where I don't think I can control the outcome. If I'm out of doors and I feel my safety is threatened it can come on… If I'm in an enclosed space and don't have access to an exit it can come on… But with me it's more of a fear of losing control. In public.'

Alejandro stroked the curls back from her eyes. 'You should have told me.'

'It's a bit tricky,' she said softly, 'telling people you're not normal.'

'It's a medical condition, Lulu, not something that's a judgement on your character.'

She lowered her eyes. 'You're not the one who can't breathe—who falls down and makes a fool of herself in public.'

'Have you?'

She hesitated. 'Once. When I was sixteen. At a concert.'

'Never again?'

She shook her head. 'But I *could*,' she said.

'And this has been going on all your life?'

'No.' This was the shameful bit. This was where everything led back to, and Lulu could feel herself closing up like a fist inside.

'When I was little we used to live with my father. He used to shout all the time, and break things and hurt my mother.'

Alejandro had a peculiar quality of stillness about him. 'Did he hurt *you*?'

'Not physically, no,' she said slowly. 'My mother protected me and the boys from that, but it was like living on top of a volcano. His rages came out of nowhere.'

'He beat your mother? You *saw* him beat your mother?'

'Only once. That was when we left. That's the thing about emotional abuse—it's not like a bruise or a cut you can look at and say, "This is what is happening." It's so subtle it plays tricks with your mind. To this day Maman still struggles with blaming herself.'

'Which is why she is so protective with you?'

'She tried to protect all of us in a difficult situation. I know she did her best.'

'But it wasn't enough.'

It wasn't a question. So she told him. She told him everything. About being reluctant to go home after school, always unsure of what she would find there. How ballet classes had been her refuge. How she would take her brothers out of their beds in the middle of the night when their father came home in a mood. How she'd learned where to hide, and how to keep it all a secret at school. After all, they were middle class…they'd lived in a nice neighbourhood, where nasty, brutish things didn't happen.

'Then we were just poor,' she said, 'which was better. Because then I could tell people my parents didn't live together and my mother had to work. It felt something like normal. But I got busier with the boys, because Maman was gone all hours. I learned how to do things around the house because Félicienne couldn't.'

'I suspect you're a useful woman to have around in a crisis, Lulu Lachaille.'

She felt a little better then.

'When did the fairytale kick in?' he asked, unable *not* to stroke the curls out of her eyes.

She looked up. 'You noticed that?'

'Your mother is married to one of France's leading foreign policy advisors—a constitutional lawyer,' Alejandro responded dryly. 'It's a little hard to miss, Lulu.'

She laughed a little then, and for the first time all night Alejandro relaxed a little. It was good to hear. He threaded the fingers of one of his hands with hers, careful not to press against her cuts.

'Jean-Luc is so sweet. They met at work, you know. Maman got a law degree after she left my father, and she was working nights as a clerk in Jean-Luc's department when she spotted something about a caveat in a contract everyone else had missed. He came down to thank her personally—'

'And tripped over his feet and could hardly get the words out?'

Lulu's mouth rounded. 'How did you know?'

'I've seen your mother—she's breathtakingly beautiful. The two of you are mirror images, twenty years apart.'

'Well, yes,' said Lulu, clearly flustered, 'if you think so. Anyway, he started giving her lifts home from work, and then we got to meet him and he was so kind. I was a little afraid of grown men until he came into our lives. All I'd seen was the havoc they caused. He's been a great role model for my brothers, and he looks after Maman so beautifully.'

But no mention of *her*. Alejandro stroked her curls again. 'He must have had a seismic impact on your life?'

She nodded vigorously, as if the telling was shifting a great weight off her shoulders. She had such slender shoulders, thought Alejandro, hit by a tenderness he hadn't expected, and from what she was telling him it was a considerable weight.

'Suddenly, at fourteen, I got my own room—fit for a princess. I was sent to a good school... I could invite other girls home for the holidays. Only I didn't.' She licked her lips. 'That's when the panic attacks started.'

'*Sí*, it would have been a miracle if they hadn't.'

Her head came back and she looked at him in astonishment.

'I have good friends on active duty in the armed forces. You're describing PTSD, Lulu—it's a natural reaction to trauma.'

'That's what I've been told,' she said slowly, jolted by the realisation that he understood. It encouraged her to reveal more. 'Routine helps me. When I know what to expect I'm better able to handle things. It's why being in the chorus works for me—being part of that team, being surrounded by the other girls, doing the same thing night after night.'

'How do you get up on stage?'

'Ballet was always my refuge, but I grew too tall. My dance teacher suggested I try out as a showgirl. I wouldn't have lasted beyond the audition stage if it hadn't been for Gigi. She was trying out too and we sort of fell in together and I just stuck to her like glue. She got me through, and once it had become my routine I discovered all sorts of ways to make it work for me. I don't feel like *myself* when I'm on stage.' She eyed him covertly. 'Don't tell anyone, but sometimes I pretend to be Rita Hayworth or Miriam Hopkins and it helps.'

Alejandro had no idea who Miriam Hopkins was, but Lulu's confession had destroyed any last remnants of his pretending he wasn't involved.

'I *am* making progress,' she went on in stalwart fashion. 'I have a therapist, and we're trialling desensitisation therapy. The fact I'm even here is huge for me. When Gigi announced she was having her wedding in Scotland I saw it as my chance to make the break. I wanted to make big changes and I was willing to take risks to push my life in a different direction. That's where you came in. At the airport.'

Alejandro was suddenly seeing that entire episode from a different angle, and his own behaviour struck at him hard. 'How did you make that flight?'

'With great organisation,' she said seriously. 'I threw up twice.'

Alejandro cursed himself under his breath.

'That was why you wouldn't move seats. You couldn't.'

'I was so embarrassed.'

'And I was a Class A bastard to you on that trip.'

'No,' she said forcefully, sitting back. 'Don't you dare apologise. You treated me like a real person, Alejandro. Like a grown woman responsible for her own actions.'

'You are without doubt a grown woman, Lulu.' He plucked a piece of straw from her hair and used it as an excuse to stroke the curls out of her eyes. 'Only a grown woman could drive me as crazy as you've been doing since you stumbled into my life.'

He was looking at her as if she was amazing. As if she was something special for all the right reasons.

Lulu couldn't believe it. She wanted to cry, but then she thought of something better.

'Maybe you could treat me like a grown woman again?'

She felt confident saying it. She liked making the first move—she'd learned that the night they'd spent together in the Scottish Highlands. It gave her a feeling of womanly power as she rose up onto her knees, watching his expression as she began unbuttoning her blouse.

He could have reminded her she'd just had a panic attack.

Told her she really should be resting.

It was what her mother would have said. Even Gigi. Treating her like the invalid she wasn't.

But Alejandro didn't do any of those things.

He carefully lifted her astride him, reached around to undo her lacy white bra and gave her full tender dominion over him.

CHAPTER FOURTEEN

ALEJANDRO PUT HER on a horse the next day.

He had a small mare saddled and brought out into the home paddock, where he patiently spent time explaining what was going on in the animal's head.

'She's used to being ridden, and she likes women. I think the two of you will get on.'

Lulu stroked her neck, and when the mare swung her head around and Lulu jumped Alejandro merely tugged on the mare's mane to show her who was boss.

'She likes you.' He grinned.

Lulu stepped a little closer and tried again, rubbing her hand over the horse's flank.

'She's so beautiful.'

'Do you think you could sit on her?'

'I'll try, but I want you to take a picture with your phone—because it might be the one and only time I'm ever on a horse.'

She was nervous, but she let Alejandro give her a leg up and found herself gripping the pommel as he fitted her feet into the stirrups.

Her heart was pounding, and she'd broken into a sweat, but Alejandro stroked her thigh reassuringly.

'It's all right, girl, she won't do anything you don't like.'

'Do you mean me or the horse?'

Alejandro grinned again and gave her the reins. He took hold of the lead rope.

His eyes were serious, though, as he looked up at her. 'I won't let go, *amorcito*. I promise.'

It was a bit like standing on the deck of a boat, but Lulu found herself falling into the rhythm of the horse's gentle stroll.

'You're a natural,' Alejandro told her.

'I don't know about that. My body understands what it needs to do—it's my mind where the battle is.'

'Then we'll do this every day until your mind comes to accept it.'

'But don't you have better things to do?'

'You need routine, Lulu,' he said calmly, as if it made sense, 'so we'll make a routine for you.'

She felt a lump rise into her throat but she didn't cry.

It took several days before she was happy enough for Alejandro to let go of the leading rope. She got the mare up to a canter—and inevitably took her first spill. She was on her feet before he reached her, straightening her helmet, laughing and groaning.

The mare nudged her and Lulu stroked her neck. 'It's not your fault, girl, I got too ambitious.'

'Nothing broken?'

Alejandro had his hands all over her, checking for damage, and Lulu rather enjoyed it and put her arms around his neck.

'Nothing a bath won't fix.'

He seemed relieved she was unhurt, and slid his hands over her bottom encased in jodhpurs. 'I should probably supervise this bath...you might drown.'

'I am a notoriously bad swimmer.' She kissed him, her arms tight around his neck.

A few mornings and several falls and bruises later, in her quest to ride at least competently, Lulu awoke to hear Alejandro moving about.

She lifted her head off the pillow. It was still dark.

'Where are you going? What's happening?'

He came over to the bed and the mattress gave beside her as he sat down and bent to stroke her hair.

'It's a working day. Go back to sleep. I'll see you after breakfast.'

Lulu peered at the time glowing from the digital clock.

It was half past four. She struggled to sit up, switching on the lamp so that she could see his face.

He was fully dressed, and so beautiful her heart contracted. 'Take me with you, if I won't be in the way. I would like to see how the estate works and what you do all day.'

He stroked her bare shoulder, looked curiously into her half-asleep eyes. 'Are you sure?'

Which meant, could she cope?

Lulu sat herself up properly. 'I won't know if I don't try.' Her expression drooped. 'But I don't want to get in the way.'

A smile broke across his face. He scooped her up, bed-clothes and all.

'What are you doing?' She laughed, fighting a yawn at the same time.

'Putting you in a shower, *amorcito*. Then we're going to dress you like a gaucho.'

A very pretty gaucho, in a cotton shirt and trousers that tucked into long leather boots.

It was a long day, but then they all were—working with the horses, driving out to a horse auction some kilometres away, checking fences. Lulu remained at his side. Sometimes she stayed in the car for a while, and he didn't question her reason, but she would eventually emerge and ask questions about what he was doing.

Everywhere they went she drew stares—because he'd never brought a woman to the *estancia* after his brief early marriage, and Valentina certainly hadn't been a presence in his working life.

At the auction he stood with her on the rails, his arms either side of her.

He couldn't blame the other men for looking. Even amidst the glamorous crowd at the wedding Lulu had stood out. Her lithe height and her embracing of a timeless femininity in everything she did had made the castle a perfect setting for a girl who seemed to have one foot in the past. At a busy horse auction, amidst the dust and the gauchos, she was glorious in a stylish vintage jacket and the thirties-style cutaway pants she seemed to prefer to wear—a magical creature come among them, eyes shining, smiling radiantly and asking questions.

No one looking on would be able to tell how nervous she was.

Dios, how hadn't he noticed that about her until now? Plainly because she'd hidden it like a pro.

But she trusted him enough now to tell him her secret, and that knowledge had ramped up his possessiveness tenfold.

When she looked up at him and smiled he found he couldn't concentrate on what was going on around them. Her kiss was a sigh just below his ear, where he discovered he was ticklish, and then her head was resting against his shoulder in an attitude of trust that had another emotion thundering through him.

His arm tightened around her. Alejandro knew then that if anyone ever tried to harm her he wouldn't be responsible for his actions.

He also knew there were probably some paparazzi in this crowd. Argentina celebrated its sporting heroes. He was rarely seen with women, so he knew that if there were, his turning up at an auction with Lulu under his arm was going to cause a bit of a feeding frenzy.

It didn't matter. He'd already made his decision.

'I have to be in the States at the end of next week,' he told Lulu when she asked if his days were always this packed.

They were driving back to Luna Plateada, with the late-afternoon sun glaring off the windscreen.

'It means time away from the *estancia*, which requires me to do all I can now.'

The end of next week. They should know about her condition then. It brought Lulu up cold. She wondered if she should worry that they never talked about it. Was Alejandro avoiding the topic because he was so set against it? She wasn't exactly over the moon about the prospect of unwed motherhood at twenty-three either! Surely they should be talking about it...

'What if I'm pregnant?' she blurted out.

Alejandro lost speed.

Oui, *Lulu, start this conversation when he's driving a high-powered four-wheel drive. You'll both be killed and the problem will be most horribly solved.*

And that was when her hand slipped protectively to her belly and she realised she wasn't exactly feeling like a woman who wouldn't be going through with an unplanned pregnancy.

Alejandro changed gear, looked over at her and said calmly, 'I'll marry you.'

'You can't just say you'll marry me and leave it at that.'

Alejandro turned the steaks over, telling himself it was just a conversation.

Although he could imagine the look on the faces of quite a few of his past girlfriends on hearing this. Sheer disbelief for one thing.

'I don't want a shotgun marriage,' she said firmly.

'No one is pointing a gun at me, *querida*.'

Lulu worried at her bottom lip and said, 'Actually—'

He looked up. She was curled on one of the outdoor sofas with a lemonade, and she wore a little frown.

She was wearing some sort of print dress with a white collar that made her look as if she'd stepped out of a nineteen-thirties film. She'd tied her curls back in bunches, which was so adorable he couldn't stop looking at her.

He was yet to see her in a pair of jeans, or in anything you could call casual or unisex.

'Should I expect one of your brothers to come bursting through the door?'

'Georg and Max? No, they wouldn't care,' she said, sounding affectionate. 'They're busy with their own lives.'

Alejandro frowned. 'They *should* care. You're their sister. You're their responsibility.'

Lulu wasn't entirely sure how she felt about the term 'responsibility', but she liked it that he cared. 'Is that how you are with *your* sisters?'

He made a grunting sound and Lulu climbed to her feet and went over to him, because this was a side of him she hadn't seen before. The growly big brother.

'I don't want any kid of mine growing up where I can't see him or her every day. Children need two parents.'

She couldn't argue with him. 'What were yours like?'

'Not great. My father was a gambler—and not a clever one. He spent most of his inheritance on the gaming tables, or on women who weren't my mother.'

'I'm sorry,' said Lulu. 'That can't have been fun for you or your sisters.'

He leaned back, folding his arms, a bottle of beer in one hand. 'I always said I'd do better by my own kids.'

'What about your *maman*?'

'She was no better. She'd arrive here with us kids and lock herself in her rooms. She was always sick unless she had a party of friends with her. We hardly ever saw her.'

'That's why you're so protective of your sisters.'

Alejandro looked uncomfortable. 'My grandfather drummed it into me—*Look after the girls...see to their interests.* And I have. But that's it. I don't interfere in their lives.'

Lulu wondered at that and drew a little closer. 'What do you mean?'

'They have their lives and I have mine. We don't live in each other's pockets.'

Given that was exactly what *they'd* been doing for the last couple of weeks, Lulu felt something lodge uncomfortably at the base of her throat.

'You like your own space?' she said slowly, giving him exactly that, edging her bottom away against the table.

'It's suited me up until now.'

Lulu tried not to take that personally. 'Would you like to have more to do with your sisters?'

He swigged at the beer, looking markedly uncomfortable. 'With me in their lives things can only end in tears. I'm there if they get into trouble, but that's about it.'

'I would have loved to have had an older brother to lean on a little,' Lulu confessed. 'I always felt like a second mum to my brothers. I think your sisters are very lucky.'

Colour actually scored the high ridge of his cheekbones. 'It's my *job*.'

Lulu felt a little sliver of cold run down her spine. Was that what his *I'll marry you* notion was about? *All* it was about? He felt *responsible*?

'You don't love them? Your sisters?'

'What kind of a question is that?'

'A simple one—it's either yes or no.'

She held his gaze, knowing that this didn't have much to do with his siblings. She wanted to hear him say it. To her. Or at least she wanted to know if there was a possibility he could love *her*.

Because that was the only reason she could see to get married. She believed in romantic love—even if she'd always imagined it wasn't something that would ever happen for her.

'Of course I love them,' he said simply. 'They're my sisters.'

'Then why would you being in their lives end in tears?'

'It's complicated, Lulu.'

'Possibly…' She looked up at him expectantly.

He made a timeless male gesture of exasperation. 'I inherited the *estancia*…the girls received dowries. They both wanted a say in the ranch—I didn't think that was a good idea. Satisfied?'

'Oh, so it's a will thing?'

Alejandro looked taken aback. 'A *will thing*?'

'Like in *King Lear*—your father hung the ranch over your heads and the child who flattered him the most got it all. Although in your case you just had to be a boy.'

'My grandfather was King Lear. He disinherited my father in favour of *me*.'

Lulu realised she'd gone stomping unaware into a minefield. Alejandro looked grim.

'How did your father feel about that?' she asked, more circumspectly.

'He never spoke to me again.'

'Oh, Alejandro, that's *awful*.'

Alejandro shrugged, but the empathy in Lulu's brown eyes warmed something that had been cold inside him for a long time.

'I took control of this place at twenty, and almost lost it. My father's gambling debts had to be paid off. The girls were still at school and there were fees.'

'Your mother couldn't help?'

'She told me she'd put up with the old man for almost two decades and she wanted her share. It wasn't as if she could go out and resurrect her modelling career.'

'But couldn't she have retrained and done something else?'

Alejandro gave her an arrested look. 'She's nothing like you, Lulu. It would never have occurred to my mother to help herself—or anyone else.'

'I'm so sorry that happened to you.' Lulu was aware he'd just paid her the most enormous compliment.

She desperately wanted to wrap her arms around him, but she also didn't want to impose when he was standing there so obviously man as an island. Men did that. She'd noticed it with her brothers when they were hurting. She would wait to have her cuddle.

'It's obvious you had a lot of responsibility on your shoulders from a young age.'

He lifted those thick lashes guarding his amazing amber-brown eyes. 'From what you've said, Lulu, so did you.'

'But my mother was always there to help me.'

Alejandro acknowledged this with a slight grunt.

'My mother didn't give a damn about her kids,' he said in a low voice, chewing out the words, 'and she sure as hell didn't lift a finger to help anyone—including herself. She took her frustrations out on us. All I remember from my childhood are her threats. She'd say she wanted to leave my father—he wouldn't let her go. She'd tell me she was going to kill herself—' He ground to a halt, rolled his shoulders as if shaking it off. 'She was a nightmare,' he muttered.

'She threatened to kill herself?' Lulu tried to keep her voice even and not make a drama of this. 'Did you believe her?'

'I was a kid,' he said without inflection. 'Of course I believed her.'

'She shouldn't have put that on you. How could she do that to you and your sisters?'

'Not the girls.' His tone was flat. 'Just me.' Alejandro's hand tightened around the beer bottle and his knuckles showed white. 'I felt responsible for her, I guess. I was the one she turned to…confided in.'

'But you were a child—she should have been protecting you from all that.'

Lulu stopped, her own chest filling with cold as her own sweet, frustrating mother flared into her mind. But *her* mother had done the best she could with what she'd had. It sounded as if Alejandro's mother hadn't cared at all.

'That's right,' he said, meeting her eyes, 'and that's why I want any child of mine under my protection.'

'From me?' Lulu framed the words in a voice that suddenly sounded very far away.

He frowned and put down the bottle, his arms falling loose to his sides. 'No, Lulu, that's not what I mean.'

'It's all right,' she said faintly, backing up. 'It's not as if I haven't thought about it. How does a woman like me take care of a helpless baby?'

'The same way you've been taking care of yourself,' he said, his tone firm. 'Look at you—you're riding a horse, you've been in crowds, you're here with me now.'

Lulu tried to focus on that, but all she was seeing was herself with a tiny baby, so vulnerable and needy, and being unable to care for it.

Alejandro put his hands on her shoulders and she felt his warmth and his strength.

'You're not alone, Lulu.'

She nodded, because she knew that was what he wanted from her, but the panic she was so familiar with was stirring like a snake in the grass and she could feel herself preparing for the worst.

She grasped at the issue at hand like a drowning woman. 'What happened with your sisters?'

'They resented me inheriting the ranch, being the favourite. They were away at school when I was struggling to keep it all together.'

'You hid it from them?'

'Protected them,' he substituted.

Lulu swallowed hard. 'So you protected them but you didn't confide in them? You don't trust them?'

'I wouldn't go that far, Lulu.' His hands slid with disarming gentleness down her arms.

'But you inherited this ranch. What about them?'

'They're taken care of.' He frowned. 'Why does this bother you?'

'Because it clearly bothers *you*. Do you see them regularly?' She knew she was being incredibly intrusive, but she could still feel that surge in her panic levels, and she needed to know what his idea of a family was if he was going to throw around marriage proposals like baseball bats.

'I see them on occasion. We're all busy people.' He was frowning at her. 'I don't have a problem with my sisters, Lulu.'

'Maybe not, but you seem to think you have a responsibility to protect them despite the difficulties in your relationship, and I wonder if that's why you're talking about marriage to *me*.'

'Lulu, if I'm going to be a father I don't have much choice.'

So there it was. She hit out at him. 'You've been married before and it didn't last,' she said.

'I was a kid. I wanted some stability and normality.' He snorted. 'It went to hell in a hand basket, naturally. It couldn't ever have been anything other than a disaster. At that age it's hard to be tied down.'

'You weren't faithful to her?' Lulu didn't really want to know.

'She cheated on *me*.'

That brought her up short.

'But—but why?'

Maria had brought out the rest of their meal, but Alejandro remained where he was.

'Valentina married me to get away from her domineering father and then discovered she'd swapped one ranch for another.'

'You rescued her,' Lulu said dully as it all fell into place. His sisters. His wife. *Her?*

'No, Lulu, I was nineteen and horny and I'd seen a lifetime of the havoc my father's indiscriminate whoring around had caused to our family. So I did the traditional thing and married her. But she liked the glamour, and I wasn't playing enough polo at the time to make my name. I was too busy saving this place from all the debt my father had drowned us in. So she slept with one of my teammates who *had* made his name.'

How any woman could exchange Alejandro for another man baffled Lulu.

'So there you have it, Lulu. The man who just proposed marriage to you. Quite a catch.'

She didn't know what to say.

'But, really, how unlucky could we be?' he went on.

Her eyes went up to meet his. She was not sure at first what he was referring to. As the penny dropped she realised he had referred to their situation in the same bored dismissive tone he'd used to impart the sorry story of his upbringing and early marriage.

Something primal stirred inside her. This wasn't a part of that. Everything in her rebelled against it.

This was real and special and he had no right to bring it down to the common denominator of those women who had failed him so fundamentally.

She wouldn't fail him.

Which was when Lulu realised she was in a lot deeper with him than she'd understood going into this conversation.

He carried the steaks over to the table. It all looked beautiful. There was even candlelight. But Lulu had never felt less like sitting down with him.

Alejandro might not have phobias to hide from, but he was carrying some serious damage from his parents. Yet he'd managed to get on in life and achieve so much in such a short amount of time. How? Where did he put the anger? The answer was in front of her. Into his work. Into the hours she'd seen him put in today. This was what he did. He *worked*.

She hid. He worked. What a pair they were.

A pregnant pair?

All of a sudden Lulu needed to sit down.

'What is it?'

Alejandro was at her side, all his masculine bravado in the face of his disturbing childhood recollections gone as he hunkered down beside her. He took the glass from her hand.

'I'm only twenty-three. You're a workaholic. This could be disastrous.'

Alejandro frowned. 'I shouldn't have told you all that. Lulu, it's in the past.' He cupped her face. 'That ship sank years ago—it's just wreckage floating past us.'

Us.

That was when it occurred to Lulu that this conversation had started off lightly enough, with her teasing him about a proposal he hadn't even made, and now somehow they'd both come round to the idea that it could be real.

She looked into Alejandro's eyes and saw her own amazement reflected back at her. Something inside her had soared over the last weeks, because he'd seen the worst of her and he hadn't run.

She thought of all the things he'd told her. She wouldn't run either.

Lulu came downstairs the next afternoon feeling confident that she looked her best in a backless raspberry silk dress worn over flowing white silk pants and a pair of thirties cream-and-black heels with perfect bows.

She knew from all Alejandro had told her that the match today, at the Campo de Buenos Aires, was one of the most important in the polo calendar. The dress code was 'cocktail', but there would be countless beautiful women and press photographers and she was nervous. She didn't want to be feeling like the odd one out. So she'd gone for glamour—a red lip and a light hand on the mascara—and teased her hair so that her curls were crisp but not overdone. She'd attached a matching silk rose to her hair with a clip instead of wearing a hat.

All in all she felt ready to face the international jet set and not disgrace herself.

Alejandro was in shirtsleeves and jeans. She knew he'd be changing into his gear at the Campo and afterwards into more formal wear for the reception.

Her breath, however, did catch as he came towards her, caught anew by his rugged looks.

'You'll be travelling separately from me, Lulu. I've got a car waiting for you now.'

'Separately? Why?'

'The press—paparazzi. With the guest list, two royal princes in attendance and a couple of half-dressed rock stars it will be wall-to-wall.'

'But they won't be interested in *me*.'

'Trust me on this, Lulu, you need to go in privately.'

'*Très bien,*' she said at last, moistening her lips and reaching up to brush the hair off his forehead. 'Well, when will I see you?'

'I'll find you. Don't worry—I'm sending Xavier with you. He won't leave your side.'

'Okay.' She wasn't sure if she was happy he was giving her a bodyguard, but she guessed she'd rather have someone to help her navigate the ground than go alone.

The last three weeks had been the happiest of her life. Alejandro had taken her with him wherever he went and, although she'd kept close to him, she had grown accustomed to the open spaces around her and was secure in the knowledge nothing was going to come cycloning out of that endless blue horizon to sweep her up.

If it did Alejandro would probably punch it.

The thought made her smile as she headed for the car.

The horse-riding lessons had developed into her doing a little gentle riding up and down the corral every day. He'd taken her about Luna Plateada in a Jeep, introduced her to the hands, to the gauchos, to the rhythms of the life they lived here.

She had seen that his heart was not so much with the *estancia* but with the horses and the breeding programme.

Besides the Criollos he had interests in a stud in the Caucasus, with Khaled Kitaev, where they were breeding mountain Kabardins.

She'd spent many nights lying beside him, listening to him musing over breed characteristics. She knew more about the oestrous cycles of mares than she really thought she ought to. But she liked the way he grew so passionate on the subject—as if it had his heart and soul in a way she suspected neither polo nor this ranch did.

The ranch was something he held in trust for the next generation.

It wasn't really about him.

Polo, she suspected, was his stress-breaker.

It was the horses that mattered—they were his passion.

As she was driven past the stables and they headed out for the highway Lulu pressed her hot cheek to the cold glass of the window and let the truth sink through her.

She was in love with him, and the only thing that mattered now was working out how to make this work.

CHAPTER FIFTEEN

As HE ATTACHED his gear Alejandro was only too aware of the crowds outside. He couldn't stop thinking about Lulu. Out there. Possibly in the sick bay. He blanked it and told himself she was in good hands with Xavier. If she was feeling in any way under pressure she would do what she needed to do. If he'd learned anything it was that Lulu was superb at self-care.

But he hadn't been parted from her for even a day since he'd brought her to the *estancia*, leaving aside the twenty-four hours he'd spent in Buenos Aires at the beginning of her visit, and it felt a little strange to be on his own again.

Weird.

He focused on what he needed to do, but in the back of his mind as he cruised the stable where his mounts were tethered he knew these last three weeks had been the best of his life.

When Khaled had rung and said he was getting married he'd thought his old friend was *loco*. But right now he understood that psychology. Keeping Lulu on a short leash appealed greatly, and putting a ring on her finger was the best way of ensuring that. She was definitely an old-fashioned girl. A wedding ring would have special properties for her. She wouldn't stray. She would stay with him. He could have her for ever.

Only experience told him that nothing lasted. Not mothers or wives. You thought you had something in your grasp, but if it didn't want to stay you had nothing.

The night after Lulu's confession in the stables he'd asked her over an alfresco dinner on the terrace how she managed at L'Oiseau Bleu, and he'd put the information she'd given him into practice.

'When I started, I had Gigi with me. We learned about the place together—how it works, what goes on—so there were no surprises.'

This he knew was key. Routine was everything for Lulu.

'There's a strict schedule for every show and that helps a lot. Also, you're in a team. I do have limitations, but nobody could link them to my anxiety condition.'

She'd looked so serious about this he had immediately wanted to confront anyone who questioned her over it.

'As it is, I've been offered solo roles so many times I can't count, and the money would be so much better.' She'd given a little Gallic shrug. '*Mais cela est impossible!* I feel more comfortable in the chorus line. Besides—' She'd broken off, suddenly looking a little shy.

'Besides...?'

'The solo roles are nude.'

'Nude?' Alejandro had put down his knife and fork. 'You mean you go on stage...?'

'Topless.'

'Naked,' he'd said at the same time.

Lulu had thrown her napkin at him. 'Don't be ridiculous—what kind of stage show would have naked women?'

Alejandro could have named several, but he hadn't been prepared to risk Lulu throwing something more substantial at him.

He'd cleared his throat. 'I was given to understand you all performed topless.'

'Not at all.'

She'd looked so cross his heart had stumbled. She'd told him once before that she wasn't topless on stage, and he realised he hadn't entirely believed her. He hadn't then—but he did now. Lulu didn't lie. She was almost painfully honest and that was part of why he'd fallen in love with her. She meant what she said.

A woman who meant what she said and did what she said. He waited to feel that old trapped feeling, as if the jaws of some mechanism were closing down on him.

He thought of his mother, railing against the hand life had dealt her. His father, flickering in and out of their lives, as insubstantial a male role model as you could imagine with his string of young girlfriends. His ex-wife, complaining about how he'd trapped her, and that moment of horror when he realised he'd married a woman startlingly like his mother.

He'd vowed he would never be like his father, and he'd held to that. Lulu was with him now because he wouldn't visit *his* childhood on any other kid. Especially a kid of his own.

Only that was just a part of the picture.

He knew now why he'd brought Lulu with him to Buenos Aires. Because she wouldn't do any of those things the people who had been supposed to love him had done.

She wouldn't cheat and lie and walk away.

Because she loved him.

She wouldn't be here, curled in his bed every night, if she didn't love him.

And that was when, like a herd of unbroken Criollos thundering across the plains of his barren heart, it all fell into place.

It wasn't until she saw the wives and girlfriends of the players being photographed with their significant others before the match that Lulu experienced the first drop of cold doubt.

Then, between chukkas, she saw Alejandro being photographed with two socialites, and when she asked questions of Xavier the poor guy tried to distract her by taking her to pet the ponies.

Honestly!

But she didn't feel confident enough to stalk across the ground, push those two girls onto their behinds and stick a passionate kiss on Alejandro—as well as sticking her heel into his foot!

Instead she stood with her glass of champagne and her smile, sat in her box during the match, decided what 'separate entrances' really meant and began to feel sick.

It all made a horrible kind of sense: if she wasn't pregnant, he didn't want their relationship to seem official in front of the world.

Lulu told herself not to be silly, not to jump to conclusions. But why else would he do this? Was he ashamed of her? Was it because she was a showgirl and he was a sixth generation du Crozier?

She set her chin mutinously. What was so hot about being descended from a horse-stealing profiteer anyway?

Only she lost her hold on her anger as Alejandro and his team thundered up and down the field. She caught her breath every time he swayed low in his saddle. She knew he wouldn't fall—she knew intellectually he was the best player on the field. But her heart still sat in her throat and she was relieved when the last goal was scored and the victory cup was filled with champagne.

'What do we do now?' she asked Xavier, who had been flirting with a very pretty blonde girl and now turned back to her with 'duty' written all over his face.

'It's all right,' she interrupted him as he began to say something about going to the marquee. 'Why don't you enjoy yourself here a little longer? I'll just pop off to the ladies'.'

Xavier didn't argue with her, and she made her way determinedly towards the sponsor's marquee.

The pitch was crowded, and there was a great deal of jostling, but she focused on her outcome—which was finding Alejandro.

She saw him with two of his teammates. They were laughing, and Alejandro had the cup under his arm.

It was as she raised her hand to catch his attention that a woman standing beside her with glorious sunshine-blonde hair turned to her and said, 'Don't even try, honey. There's a queue for Alejandro du Crozier and the competition is fierce.'

'Pardon?'

But the woman had already turned to her companion and forgotten about her.

Lulu blinked and swallowed.

'Lulu!' Alejandro had finally seen her and was shouldering his way towards her like the force of nature he was.

Somehow she'd forgotten in the last weeks who he was, his reputation, and the very public life he led.

The public life he'd sidelined her from.

Why?

What was wrong with her?

Why did that woman think she couldn't cut it with the competition?

She looked up at him and some of her distress must have been in her eyes, because he frowned. But then he caught her around the waist and lifted her with both hands. Instinctively she put her arms around his neck and then he was kissing her—deeply, passionately—and she kissed him back—furiously, possessively.

After almost a month with Alejandro she had massive skills in kissing!

As her heels touched the ground again a little light applause broke out around them.

Lulu didn't even care. She had her arm around him, and he was hot and sweaty, and he was hers.

'Come on,' he said, 'walk me to the showers.'

Twilight was gathering outside. People called out to him, but apart from lifting his hand to give a brief wave he ignored them, steered her off, away from the official crowd, towards the players' amenities.

Lulu was full of mixed emotions. She didn't understand what had gone down today but she knew it was crucial to whatever was between them.

'Alejandro, why did I have to arrive separately? Nobody knew who I was. One woman told me I didn't have a chance with you.'

'*Que?*' Anger rippled across that steady surface she depended on. 'What woman?'

'I don't know—some woman. Are there a lot of groupies?'

'*Sí.*' He stopped and pulled her in against him. 'But that doesn't affect us.'

'Well, it does if no one knows who I am.'

He frowned. 'It won't happen again.'

'It wouldn't have happened at all if you'd let me arrive with you, like a normal couple—like everyone else,' she finished, feeling she was whining but not knowing any other way to put it.

He studied her face. 'Look, I'll be honest with you. I arranged for you to enter privately because I was concerned you would have a panic attack. I didn't want to put you through that level of anxiety.'

She shook her head. 'But I wouldn't—I mean I thought you understood.'

'Understood *what*, Lulu?'

He looked faintly irritated. Or it might be that he was just tired. It had been a hard match, and he still had to shower and change and talk to the sponsors and the media and… And she was holding him up.

'This is what you do, isn't it? You fly around the world and play polo for six months of the year.'

'*Sí.*'

'So every time you play I'll have to be secreted away?'

He released a gusty sigh. 'Once we get you into a routine it won't be a big deal, but until then you need to be careful.'

'Why? Because I'll embarrass you?'

'Because, *mi chica loca*, I can't keep my mind on the match if I'm worrying about you.'

Lulu flinched. She knew enough Spanish now to know he'd called her his crazy girl. She tried not to let that get its teeth into her. 'You're right,' she said heavily. 'I didn't think of that.'

His expression softened and he framed her face with his hands, stroked her hair as if he needed to touch her.

'It will get better, Lulu. *You* will get better.'

She knew then, even if he hadn't faced it, that she couldn't fit into his lifestyle. Alejandro was operating on a timescale that ended with her getting better. She was never going to get better. Even if she hadn't discussed this with her therapist she would have known it on a gut level herself. Some things you just had to learn to live with and, where you could, embrace them.

Alejandro had made her comfortable within her limitations, but he was waiting for her to 'get better'.

Suddenly her path became terrifyingly clear. 'I'm going back to Paris. Tonight.'

'Hang on—what?' He looked genuinely thrown.

'The new season for our show starts up next week, I'd have to go by Monday anyway. You know I have a job.'

'I don't want you to go.' He spoke as if this were a fact. Not a request. He seemed to realise this, because he exhaled a breath and said more reasonably, 'Listen, I don't know where all this has come from, but I think you're having a reaction to the stress of the day—'

'No!' She exploded in a low roar, yanking herself free of him. 'You do *not* speak to me like that, Alejandro. I am *not* crazy—do you understand me? I came here with you to Buenos Aires because I was scared and I thought it was the right thing to do.'

She frowned, because that wasn't entirely true. She'd come because she'd wanted something with him, and for the last couple of weeks she'd thought she'd found it. Had it all been a fantasy? Cooked up by a combination of her tendency to cling to people who offered her support and her inexperience with men so she hadn't understood she was fooling herself?

'I thought it was the right thing to do,' she repeated. 'Instead we've just confused the issue.'

'I'm not confused, Lulu.'

'Well, I am! Do you know what a baby would mean for me? It would mean dismantling all the new stuff I've been putting in place to try and make my own life. It would mean no downsizing to a flat I can afford to pay for, no starting college, no career that I've been dreaming of. All the things I've been working so hard towards—to make myself independent—would be taken away.'

It all came pouring out, and that was when Lulu realised what she feared was not her ability to rise to this very grown-up challenge, but that she was going to lose her options.

That she would be handing over responsibility for her life to Alejandro and nothing about her would have changed.

'If feels like all my life I've been losing ground, inch by inch. I want my life to *open up*, Alejandro, not close down.'

She shut her eyes, because she knew how she sounded. Selfish. Self-centred. All the horrible things he'd once said she was.

'But I know one thing,' she whispered. 'If I'm pregnant I don't want to be making choices out of fear. Part of me wants you to wave a wand and make it all work—absolve me from being a bad person who feels angry and resentful that her life choices are being taken away from her. Again.'

It was the 'again' that silenced Alejandro when he would
have argued with her.

He couldn't do it to her. If she felt trapped the last thing
he should do was clang those bars shut.

A dark tide of bitterness came, moving up through him.
He'd been blind. *Again.*

She gave him a sorrowful look. 'You're thirty-two.
You've been married and divorced, you've carved out a
successful career and you run a working *estancia*. There's
nothing you can't do, Alejandro. And I've done what? Held
down a chorus role in the Bluebirds. I'm not ready to have
a baby,' she choked.

It was a relief to say it. It was also incredibly painful,
because she knew now she was going home without him.

He placed a hand that was incredibly gentle on her shoulder, but his eyes—they looked dead. Her heart stuttered.

'I will phone you as soon as I have the results,' she said,
making herself hold his eyes.

'I want to fly you back to Paris,' he said quietly in return.

She started. 'N-no. I can fly by myself.'

Let me be normal! she wanted to yell, until it splin-
tered the air, but who was she railing against? Alejandro?
Herself?

'You need someone to travel with you. Let me organise
that, at least. I want you to feel safe.'

Lulu felt it like a punch to her chest.

After everything that had happened over the last few
weeks he still saw her as crippled. Just like everyone else.
She knew then that she was doing the right thing—no matter how much she was hurting.

'I am capable of boarding a flight alone,' she said, in a
voice that felt wrung out with yelling, although neither of
them had raised their voices.

He was being so appallingly reasonable—and quiet.

'Lulu—'

She knew the words that would stop him in his tracks

but it would hurt like razor blades bloodying her mouth to utter them.

'Don't you understand, Alejandro? *I don't want you*.'

She turned around and walked. Very fast. Very deliberately. She knew after those words that Alejandro would not follow.

CHAPTER SIXTEEN

IT HAD BEEN six weeks. Summer had turned to autumn and leaves rolled along the Paris street as Alejandro parked his hire car and looked up at the unexceptional six-storey building wedged between a laundromat and a thriving North African restaurant.

He checked the address. This was it.

Pocketing the car keys, he went inside and took the stairs up four flights.

He was ringing her bell when he realised this couldn't be the flat her parents had paid for.

Lulu was living within her own means.

He recognised that this wasn't going to be as easy as he'd thought.

If she'd put her plans into action she might be less inclined to give him a hearing. Plus, he was still angry with her. It burned more the closer he got to this moment, seeing her again, when he knew she damn well didn't want to see him.

Well, he wasn't giving her a choice. He knew Lulu. She'd only run and hide. The memory of her hunched over and trembling behind that nineteenth-century desk flashed unexpectedly to mind, but he shoved it aside. Thinking of Lulu small and fragile and vulnerable only got him so far. She wanted him to see her as strong. He'd treat her that way.

The sound of a dog barking preceded the door opening. She had at least four chains on it, which satisfied his desire for her to be safe but also had him wondering about the neighbourhood.

The door swung open and his pulse sped up.

It was Lulu. In soft blue leggings, a stripy pullover, and she was holding a fluffy black dog in her arms.

Her hair was longer. Her eyes looked bigger—as if she'd lost weight.

Or maybe it was because she was staring at him.

She was so beautiful.

All his anger fell away.

'Alejandro?'

She looked as if she was seeing a ghost and it occurred to him that he should have rung. But it hadn't been common sense that had seen him walk out of a sponsor's event in Connecticut and take a flight direct to Paris this morning. It had been the certainty that if he didn't claim her now she would never be his.

'Lulu.' His usual smooth charm with the female sex had deserted him and he was lost for words.

She looked so delicate—nothing like the determined and robust picture she'd built for him over the phone.

Because she'd rung him to confirm that she wasn't pregnant.

He'd had a moment when disappointment had bloomed so hard and fast in his chest he hadn't been able to speak.

She'd repeated his name and he'd found the appropriate words—it was good news…she must be relieved—and said he wanted to come and see her.

She hadn't spoken again, and it had been the longest moment, stretching between them across continents.

He had been in London, she here in Paris. Obviously in this depressing-looking little flat.

'I don't know if that's a good idea,' she'd said at last, in a small voice.

He hadn't pushed then, because he'd learned not to push. It was why he had never made an effort to be in his sisters' lives.

He'd kept thinking about what Lulu had said about loving his sisters, about trusting them. That was why a few weeks ago he'd invited the girls to join him in London. It had been a good weekend—catching up, sharing news. And he was currently drawing up a contract to give the girls equal shares in Luna Plateada. It was something long overdue.

'What are you doing here?' Lulu said now, her eyes fixed on his.

Good question. He should have been here six weeks ago. Instead he'd been touring with the team. Going to bed at night at ten, getting up before dawn, blocking what was standing in front of him now from his mind. He'd been gently mocked by a couple of his teammates and friends for eschewing the nightlife that went along with a tour. He'd had no interest in other women.

He was looking at the reason why.

'Are you free for dinner?'

She looked flummoxed. 'I have a show tonight, I'm not off until after eleven.'

No other man, then. He could feel the knot of tension he'd carried in his gut these past weeks easing.

Or at least not tonight. Tomorrow—who knew? Paris was a big city. He could imagine hundreds of worthy men lining up to take her out to dinner, to set aside the doubts and fears he'd held on to too long. One of those men would put a ring on her finger.

'I'll pick you up.'

'I don't know, Alejandro…' she said slowly.

'You're so busy with this new life of yours you can't date?'

She moistened her lips, widened her eyes slightly. 'Is this a date?'

'What else would it be?'

'You want to *date* me?'

'Indisputably.'

She hesitated. 'Just because you're in Paris tonight?'

He knew then he had a lot to prove. 'No, *amorcito*, I'm here because *you're* in Paris.'

* * *

It was bedlam.

The new girl from Australia, Romy, had pulled a hamstring in the last number and was in too much pain to perform the 'Little Egypt' set.

Anna, the *maîtresse de ballet*, was on her knees, begging Lulu to don transparent scarves and wiggle her way through the act.

'Those extra pounds on your hips can only help,' she wheedled.

'Those pounds you told me not four hours ago I was to get rid of or I'd be fined? *Those* pounds?' Lulu demanded.

Anna clambered off her knees, dusting them off. 'Well, maybe we can come to some sort of agreement.'

'Oui,' said Lulu crisply. 'A *signed* agreement, before I go on to tell you that the extra pounds are *my* business.'

'Wow, Lulu, what happened to you in Argentina?' asked Trixie.

'The mouse roars,' said another dancer, Leah. 'We should *all* get dumped by hot polo stars, girls.'

Lulu ignored them. All she could think about was what was awaiting her tonight, when the show was over.

He'd come for her.

When her period had made an appearance the day after she'd got back she'd cried and cried, and right up until Alejandro had appeared at her door this afternoon she hadn't really known why.

At first, as she'd gone about putting into practice all her plans, she hadn't been able to work out why she wasn't relieved. It meant all her old goals were still in place—nothing had been shifted. Nothing but her.

She'd changed. Her priorities were different. She no longer felt the need to prove herself because deep down she knew now that she would make a superlative mother. If only because she would love her baby. It wouldn't be easy, but nobody's life was easy, and if she had a little more to overcome than other people it would just make her stronger, more resilient.

She could actually *see* herself as a wife and mother, see herself occupying that next stage in life. And it didn't mean giving anything up.

She'd rung Alejandro and told him the no-baby news while he'd been on tour. There had been female voices in the background and he'd told her he was in a marquee, picking up an award. He hadn't sounded very interested in it—it had only been later that she'd learned from the newspapers that he'd picked up that award from royalty.

Then he'd asked to come and see her and she'd said no.

She'd thought he was being nice. Tidying up the loose ends.

So why was he here?

She faced herself in the mirror. Why would he want to be stuck with someone like her? She might be getting better, but she was never going to be completely without her irrational fears.

Only wasn't that falling back into her old patterns of thought? She'd learned that from him—learned to catch herself at it. Alejandro had given her a release from them when he'd talked to her about her father.

He'd also given her a tool to work with.

It was that new knowledge which acted as a powerful guidance system inside her. Her daily fear of constant collapse had receded and it was allowing her to see everything a lot more clearly.

She'd told her parents her plans at her first Sunday lunch back home, and as she'd suspected her mother had had a meltdown. But Jean-Luc had overridden those objections and told her he was proud of her, that they would step aside as she wished, although if she needed them they would always be there.

Which was when she'd flung her arms around Jean Luc's neck and told him she couldn't have a better stepfather if he was Gregory Peck.

The following weeks had passed in a blur of activity. She'd watched strangers traipse through her flat and she'd wandered through other people's until she'd found one in the next *arrondissement*. It took up half of her weekly income, but it had its own bathroom, which was a plus, although no courtyard or anywhere to sit in the sun.

Still, she wasn't home much, between working nights at L'Oiseau Bleu and college starting up, and her puppy Coco had to spend more time living at her parents. *She* seemed to live on the bus between college and the cabaret.

She told herself it was true independence, but knew it wasn't going to be easy.

Nothing worthwhile ever was.

So facing down Anna hadn't really been that difficult just now. It was thinking about Alejandro and what his appearance back in her life meant that made everything ache...

'Why don't you girls all mind your own business?' said Adele suddenly. 'Worry about your own love lives or lack thereof!' She reinforced this uncharacteristic show of support by leaning down and murmuring, 'I've got your back, Lu.'

That Adele should prove to be her ally wasn't so unexpected, Lulu guessed. Since she'd stopped worrying about people discovering her condition she'd developed a backbone and had been getting a lot of the respect she'd missed out on in the past.

'Thanks, Lulu, for helping out,' Romy said, hopping over on one leg and lowering herself into a chair. 'I just keep it to a figure eight, but make sure you only drop two scarves at a time—no more, or you'll run out...'

Lulu waited for more instructions, but Romy had stopped speaking.

In fact everyone was quiet.

She looked up and everything went haywire.

Alejandro had never been backstage at a theatre.

Up until the moment he'd stepped through the stage door he had pictured L'Oiseau Bleu as a girly joint.

He hadn't been far wrong.

The first person he ran into was a topless peacock, or so she appeared to be, who shrieked, clapped her arms over her breasts—and then changed her mind, asked if he was Alejandro du Crozier, and if so could he sign her...?

Then he slammed into a stagehand who told him to go around to the front of the building and approach the booking office. No members of the public were allowed backstage during a performance.

'We've got a nudity clause,' the guy said.

'I'm not interested in the nudity. I'm looking for Lulu Lachaille,' Alejandro told him.

'You'll have to speak to the manager—'

'Who is on her honeymoon,' Alejandro cut him off.

He could hear music. Knew that elsewhere in this place there was a show going on. He wanted to get to Lulu before she hit the stage, because he had this crazy, unrealistic idea that if he didn't he would have lost her.

He couldn't wait until eleven o'clock. He'd already waited six weeks.

'I mean the *assistant* manager,' the guy fired back, looking uneasy.

'Who is...?' Alejandro was ready to slice and dice this guy.

'Alejandro du Crozier!'

He turned around. The feather-clad blonde hip-swinging towards him was vaguely familiar.

'Susie. Susie Sayers.' She gave him a speculative sweep, from his boots to the curl of his overly long chestnut hair.

He remembered. Susie. The bridesmaid with the wandering hands.

'Where is she?' he demanded without preamble.

'Come this way, gorgeous. Follow Susie!'

He followed the bouncing ostrich feather tail down a corridor, and he heard the sound of shrill female voices before he saw the dancers.

A couple of naked women shrieked, and one or two just put their hands on their hips and watched him come in.

Then he saw her.

Or he thought he saw her.

Sitting at a mirror framed with glowing bulbs, applying powder to her already luminescent skin.

'Alejandro!' She dropped the brush and swivelled around in her chair.

He couldn't get over how she looked. She was wearing a rhinestone bikini, a long ostrich feather tail and towering heels.

She was a showgirl.

Until this moment he hadn't really believed it.

'What are you doing here?'

'I came to see the show.'

'Five minutes until Little Egypt.' The announcement came over the tannoy.

'That's me.' She shimmied out of her tail in front of him, and Alejandro was confronted by Lulu's very luscious, very familiar behind in a tiny sparkly G-string.

She was going on stage in *that*?

Like hell she was!

Lulu began attaching a skirt made of scarves, her hands working fast as she arranged them.

Alejandro relaxed slightly. That was better.

'Enjoy the show,' she said, and with an entirely un-Lulu-like taunt of a smile she slipped past him.

Alejandro turned around and was confronted by a roomful of semi-naked women, all looking him speculatively up and down.

'Ladies…' he said and, feeling ridiculously objectified, waded his way out of the dressing room to find out what Lulu was up to.

He found out from the wings of the stage. Against a set he assumed was supposed to resemble nineteenth-century Egypt, Lulu swayed and manipulated her hips to the snaky, seductive music.

Ridiculous as it was, he had never actually thought about Lulu being a dancer, but her talent was evident. He couldn't take his eyes off her.

The problem was he imagined every other man in the audience was in the same predicament.

As the scarves fell away his tension grew—until there she was, virtually naked behind a semi-transparent screen. Only he could see she was wearing a flesh-coloured bikini.

And as he looked around at the faces in the audience below Alejandro realised half of them were women.

When Lulu wrapped herself in a crimson robe and came out to centre stage there was a burst of thunderous applause and he watched her take a bow, as she must do every night. Alejandro joined in with the applause—and then it occurred to him that she *didn't* do this every night and he'd just seen something extraordinary.

Lulu had performed solo.

It was a different woman he escorted into an exclusive restaurant overlooking the Luxembourg Gardens.

His gaze dropped to her bottom, now encased in a fishtailed dark purple cocktail dress, but somehow he could still see that strip of sparkles.

She had never looked more beautiful, with her skin luminescent against the coloured silk, cut modestly across her breasts, and her delicate shoulders bare beneath narrow straps.

As he seated himself opposite her Alejandro was very aware that this was how their relationship should have begun.

Dinner. Dancing. Him coming to Paris to see her again and again. Flying her down to his yacht in the Mediterranean. Looking at her through candlelight.

He drew her out on her college course, how she was juggling her two worlds, the new flat, how her parents were dealing with it, and soon her hesitant replies grew more fluid. She lost her self-consciousness and began to talk as he'd never really heard Lulu talk before. She didn't apologise for anything—she just enthused.

He'd missed her so much, and yet he knew the woman in front of him had needed that time.

'You haven't been seeing anyone since you got back?' With difficulty he kept the question neutral.

'I—I tried. I had lunch with a guy on my course.' She looked up. 'He's nice.'

'Nice?' Alejandro struggled with that concept and lost. He inhaled. 'How about me? What am I?'

'You're *you*,' she said in a quiet voice, 'and you haven't said what you thought of the show.'

'You performed solo.'

'Only under duress—but, yes, I did.' She moistened her lips. 'Nothing else has changed, Alejandro. I'm still seeing my therapist. I still sometimes can't leave the flat. On my scale I'm doing well, but my scale is much smaller than yours.'

He frowned, but was careful to keep his voice level. 'In what way?'

'When I rang you about not being pregnant you were collecting a trophy from the Prince of Wales!'

He shook his head slightly. 'And...?'

'That's your life. You're out there on the world stage and I'm... I'm on stage at L'Oiseau Bleu, still trying not to lose my lunch.'

He fingered the stem of his untouched champagne glass, his frustration building. 'I never hung our relationship on the idea that you would get better, Lulu,' he said slowly, choosing his words carefully, 'but I think *you* did.'

'What do you mean?'

'I think it's a convenient excuse for you. If you weren't "sick", as you call it, what other excuse would you use to not be with me?'

'I'm not making excuses.' She shifted in her seat, very pale now. Her mouth quivered.

'You have a kind of agoraphobia, and yet you climb on stage with the other Bluebirds every night of the week. You do it because it means so much to you. Yet you won't take the chance to have a relationship with me because I'm on the world stage? As far as I can see, Lulu, they're both stages. You choose which one you want to stand on.'

She was breathing fast. 'You're the one who won't accept me as I am.'

Alejandro held her eyes with his. He looked so incredibly calm, when she was breaking into a million pieces.

She willed him to tell her he *did* accept her. That he would move heaven and earth to be with her. And suddenly she was angry with him.

What right had he to do this to her? He should have left her alone. Instead he'd dragged her to dinner just to flay her alive.

'Can I give you an opinion you're not going to like?'

'No,' she said, in a small, tense voice.

'I think you've used your phobia in the past to keep men at arm's distance. I don't think you've allowed yourself to accept how truly frightening living with your father was.'

Lulu opened her mouth to disagree, to tell him he was way off base, only…

'You don't want to find yourself in that situation again, so somewhere inside yourself you're still that little girl, hiding away.'

She sat very still, as if he'd opened up Pandora's Box and what had jumped out was eyeing her. She found she couldn't move.

When he spoke again his voice had deepened. 'What I want to know is why me?'

She inhaled his warm, musky male scent and the answer was there before she'd even thought about it. *Because the moment I clapped eyes on you the backs of my knees went and that had never happened to me before.*

But that wasn't the only reason.

'You were so awful to me I didn't have any choice but to fight back,' she whispered.

'And you never fought back with your father, did you? You always ran away—like your mother told you to.'

She gave a slight nod, because to have done any more would have shattered her.

'So there we are. It's not fear that's holding you back, Lulu, its anger.'

The powerful wave of emotion that had been pushing its way through her body since he'd arrived on her doorstep that morning broke, and Lulu found herself scraping back her chair from the table.

Perhaps he said her name—she wasn't sure, because she was running across the restaurant. She knocked a waiter's arm and the tray he carried went smashing to the floor.

Heads turned…there was a flurry of activity around her…but Lulu couldn't stay.

'I'm sorry… I'm so sorry,' she muttered, and continued to push her way out of the restaurant.

And then she was out in the floodlit square, the autumn breeze cold on her bare arms. But there was no going back, and she ran down the street in her clumpy heels, her heart pounding.

'Lulu!'

Alejandro caught her before she could hail a taxi.

He turned her in his arms.

In that moment Lulu wanted to deny it. She wanted to shout at him that her phobias had nothing to do with her, that it was something outside of her. Something she couldn't control.

Her father.

She looked up into Alejandro's beautiful face, lined with concern for her, and knew he was right. She'd never got the chance to confront him.

'He never loved me!' she shouted, shoving Alejandro in the chest with both hands, unable even to shift him, which was hugely, crazily comforting. 'He was so full of anger he couldn't love anything. How can you say I'm like that? I'm *not*!' She stumbled back, hugging herself. 'I'm not like that, am I?'

And there it was—her greatest fear. She wasn't loveable. There was something intrinsically wrong with her.

The girl with the madman for a father.

The question was like a knife she'd put to her own throat.

'No,' he said in a hoarse voice, stepping up to her, laying that knife down. Offering his large body as both punching bag and shelter. 'You're not filled with anger, Lulu, you're *angry*. There's a difference.'

He put his arms around her and this time she didn't fight. This time she let him tighten his arms around her.

'You have a right to be angry, *amorcito*,' he said, his mouth warm against her temple.

She clung to him, not caring that they were in the middle of a public place, taking all the skin-on-skin contact she could get from him. And if a small part of her wondered where private, buttoned-up Lulu had got to, the rest of her knew.

Her family wouldn't recognise her.

Nobody would. Only Alejandro.

He had undone all her buttons from the very beginning. This was the last one.

'You *should* be angry,' he reiterated.

She clutched at him—not because she was frightened, but because she felt that she could.

She didn't have to hide her feelings any more.

'I was never allowed to be angry with my mother,' he told her, his mouth at her ear. 'That's why I know how you feel. And because of that I almost lost you. That morning when you told me you didn't want to see me again I was reacting to old anger, Lulu. And if we hadn't gone to the castle…if I'd flown off in the other direction…'

'But you didn't.' She framed his face with her hands. 'You stuck around. You made me face you. You made me faces my fears.'

'You don't have to be afraid any more, little Lulu,' he said, with infinite understanding.

And Lulu let herself unravel some more, and when he put her in a taxi with him and tucked her against him she began to feel maybe she didn't.

He took her back to her flat but they didn't stay there. He had understood she would want her little dog Coco with her—her *toutou*—and he was all they collected.

The staff at the Paris Ritz didn't blink an eye as Lulu, still in her cocktail dress, carried her small bichon in her arms across the lobby like a queen. Because this was Paris, and they understood the importance of companion animals, and Alejandro du Crozier was a rich and famous guest and he could do what he liked.

In his bedroom she turned in his arms and kissed him, stroked him with a fervour she had never shown before, and he wanted her so badly his body felt on fire.

Lying in his arms, Lulu just looked at him, with those big brown eyes full of all the sweetness and stubbornness, hopes and fears her heart harboured. And Alejandro saw himself reflected in them, and he knew then it really had been love at first sight.

He'd walked down that aisle, on that fateful flight from

Heathrow to Edinburgh, and all she'd had to do was lift those big eyes.

Sí, definitely hooked.

'I love you,' she said simply. 'You know I do.'

He did. He swallowed hard, because it seemed he'd waited his whole life to hear those words from this woman.

'I want a ring,' she said seriously. 'I'm not just moving in with you.'

'Naturally.'

And then he gathered her up in his arms and just held her, and a great peace came over him because she loved him.

Neither of them was trapped. It was the lack of love that made you feel trapped.

They loved one another enough to defeat anything that might stand in the way of them being together.

'And, Alejandro...?' Lulu said, hugging him back.

'Yes, my love?'

'I'm planning on a big fairytale wedding. We might need a castle too...'

* * * * *

If you enjoyed this novel,
you can read Gigi's story:

CAUGHT IN HIS GILDED WORLD

Available now!

MILLS & BOON®

MODERN™

POWER, PASSION AND IRRESISTIBLE TEMPTATION

MILLS & BOON®

The Irresistible Greeks Collection!

You'll find yourself swept off to the Mediterranean with this collection of seductive Greek heartthrobs. Order today and get two free books!

Order yours at
www.millsandboon.co.uk/irresistiblegreeks

0516_IG

MILLS & BOON®

Mills & Boon have been at the heart of romance since 1908... and while the fashions may have changed, one thing remains the same: from pulse-pounding passion to the gentlest caress, we're always known how to bring romance alive.

Now, we're delighted to present you with these irresistible illustrations, inspired by the vintage glamour of our covers. So indulge your wildest dreams and unleash your imagination as we present the most iconic Mills & Boon moments of the last century.

Visit **www.millsandboon.co.uk/ArtofRomance**
to order yours!